A TOUCH OF AUTHORITY

B. B. Rattan

To Terry. Chastity's a bitch.

CHAPTER ONE

Submissive Initiates

Delia D'Morn walked along the trail, bundled against the cold in tall, thick socks, brown boots, a long, cotton tunic, and a wool cloak that came down to her knees and buckled up the front. Her hands were covered in leather gloves, which in turn were covered in woolen mitts. The double layers were necessary to keep her fingers from going numb. Between the tunic and the cloak, a thick shawl—more like a blanket—was wrapped around her shoulders. Part of the shawl was pulled up out of the coat and wrapped around the lower part of her face to protect her mouth and nose. She also wore a smaller wrap around her ears, but it was covered by the hood of the cloak.

The others from her circle walked in a group around her—some before and some behind—all walking along the same trail and wearing similar garments.

As she walked, Delia tried to keep her head down to keep the shawl from slipping off her nose, and to keep the wind out of her eyes. It wasn't working out for her. She preferred to see where she was going and what was going on around her at all times. Although she'd walked this path many times, she couldn't help lifting her head to get a better view, and inevitably, the shawl would slip below her nose, leaving the upturned little nub subject to the burning cold of the wind.

Occasionally, as she walked, she would try to pull the warm wool back up over her face to give her freezing nose some respite.

The day was not sunny. She preferred the sunny cold days. Even if it was cold, the sun made the day feel more bearable. Today, instead, it was gray and cloudy. She hadn't noticed the snow from her window this morning, but on this path through the woods, she could see a light sprinkling of snowflakes, barely visible. She looked around at her fellow initiates and wondered if any of the others noticed it. Their heads all pointed down toward the ground, trying to keep the wind out of their faces, but the snow was not piling up there. It was too sparse.

Kondari was always telling them to be observant of what was around them—that they could always find something new even in a familiar place—and Delia felt smug that she had noticed the tiny snowflakes that probably none of the other initiates in her circle had seen. They were not walking, however, with Kondari, the Instructor of the Philosophy of Submission. At the head of their procession, instead, was Pehr, Instructor of Pain Processing.

Pehr was a sweet-looking woman in her early fifties. She was short—though not quite as short as Delia, herself—and had bobbed, curly gray hair with messy, curly bangs at the front. Pehr's body was soft and plump. And she was the premier expert in her field. Like many of the instructors in the College of Submission at DS Academy, Pehr, herself, was a submissive. The tales of Instructor Pehr's ability to withstand pain were legendary among the students.

When they reached the clearing about two miles into the woods, Pehr had them stop and form up in a rough circle, making room for each initiate. Delia shifted her weight back and forth from one foot to the other, trying to keep her body moving and generating heat.

"We have come to this clearing to meditate." Pehr looked around the circle at the initiates. Delia watched the others' faces, too. A few seemed resigned to the idea of sitting on the ground in the cold. They began to lower themselves. Others looked put off at the announcement, but when they saw their companions preparing for meditation, they too began to lower their bodies to the ground.

Pehr of course saw the looks on the faces of those who didn't like the idea. Pehr saw everything. Before most of the initiates had even lowered themselves to a seated position, the instructor explained the activity further. "Before you begin meditating, each of you must undress." Shock was clear even on the faces of those who had at first resigned themselves to the idea of sitting in the cold.

They were all layered and well-protected, and even so, the cold was not entirely comfortable. Delia and the others had spent the whole walk trying to keep the wind off their faces, which had been the only exposed skin on their bodies. Some of the initiates wore faces of outright indignation. Pehr turned to one of those. The one she turned to just happened to be Delia's friend, Meela.

"Your face does not look like the face an initiate in the school of submission," the instructor snapped.

Meela replaced the look of indignation with downturned eyes. Delia, for her part, had already started removing her clothes. She was always eager to please. To stand out from the other initiates. And she was good at pain processing class. She started with the hood. The wind bit into her cheeks the moment it was down. Then she removed the cloak and shawl. They were her warmest layers, and she was already shivering, even with her clothes still on. She took off her boots, and one by one she removed all the layers beneath. She saved the tall, warm socks for last, and stood in the socks, clasping her hands around her upper arms as though she could keep herself warm.

Already the wind bit into her body. All of her skin hurt. That was the worst part about being cold. Low temperatures didn't bother her as long as all of her skin was covered. She looked down at the socks. She hated for her toes to be cold. She took a deep, calming breath and pried her hands loose from herself. She lowered herself to the ground, where beneath her buttocks she felt damp, frosty moss and hard-packed dirt. Initiates in the College of Submission got used to being dirty sometimes. Once seated, Delia looked around at the other initiates. They were all still in various states of undressing, and there were many different types of bodies beneath the homogenous bundles of clothing.

Her eyes caught on one initiate whose body was much different from hers. It always amazed her how much variety people came in. This woman had long, rich, black hair. She was tall—much taller than Delia. And she had big, hanging breasts, thighs that pressed into each other, and a soft, squishy belly. Delia knew from her Introduction to Fetishes class that women with this body type were highly desirable by several groups of Dominants.

Delia's body type had also been discussed in that course—and fit into a much different category, no less sought after, though Delia had at first been uncertain about some of the implications. She was small all around, with small tits, a short stature, and a tiny waist. The only thing not tiny about her was her plump bottom.

She turned her attention back to her task and peeled one sock down her leg, the material bunching up at the ankle. Then she grabbed it by the toe and pulled the whole length of sock off her foot. She did the same with the other, placing them on top of the pile of clothes next to her.

Her teeth chattered, and her cunt felt like she'd pressed it against an ice block. Still, it was the warmest place on her body. She could feel her cunt radiating heat, and she tucked her hands between her legs, trying to regain some feeling in her fingertips. Her whole body was shaking, and now that she was unclothed, she was intensely aware of her vaginal secretions. The fluid caught the cold air, causing her to feel the wind's chill more intensely on her most delicate bits, and her body responded to the sensation only by creating more secretions. She shifted uncomfortably on her bottom.

Delia tried to divert her attention away from the pain of the wind biting her skin by looking around at her companions. Most of the other initiates were also women, but a few in her circle were men, and Kapp—small and muscular—was an enby. All of them looked miserable, rocking forward and back, shivering, hugging themselves, and covered in goosebumps.

"Now that all of you are undressed, you have five minutes of meditation to complete." Pehr stood at the center of the circle, turning to examine each of the submissive initiates. "You will masturbate to help you cope with the pain."

No one moved.

"Masturbate now," Pehr said.

Delia didn't particularly feel like masturbating, and she suspected none of the other initiates did either, but she wiggled one finger between the folds of her labia and found that at least it was warmer in there. She focused on that warmth. One of the male initiates was rubbing his cock, but it didn't seem to be responding to the stimulus. She turned to look at her friend, Meela. Despite their constant exposure to the eyes of others, Meela still wasn't comfortable with people watching her perform sexual acts. Her friend was making the tiniest movements possible with one fingertip against her clit.

Delia felt a little sorry for her friend. Meela was conventionally beautiful. She was of medium height with medium, olive skin that looked like it had a perpetual light tan. She had a build that was pleasantly curvy in both the butt and the boobs while also having a flat tummy. Meela's hair was long, dark, and wavy; her face, perfectly proportioned with a dainty nose, lips that were full—yet not too full—and striking, green-gray eyes.

Meela would likely have no problem finding a Dominant who would take her after graduation. Many of them looked for a few conventional beauties to add to their households. The problem was that the more interesting positions generally called for a submissive who fit a particular fetish. Conventional beauties often ran the risk of being taken in by Doms with little imagination—those who collected beauties and then left them to languish mentally and emotionally—while the more interesting roles often went to those submissives who fit a fetish niche. Of course, women like Meela still had a chance if they chose the right major.

Pehr continued to speak to them from the center of the circle, watching each of them trying to cope with the intense pain of the cold. "Sexual stimulation is one of your greatest tools against pain. Engaging your sexual organs stimulates endorphins, but more importantly, it helps you to associate the pain with more pleasurable sensations. Eventually, you will be able to tolerate the pain without any sexual stimulation at all."

That felt hard to believe. Delia tried to ignore the fact that she could no longer feel her toes by stroking her finger between the folds of her inner labia. It was still warm in there. She drew her mind to that inner warmth and began rubbing her clit. It was hard to do with numb fingers. She switched tactics, pressing a couple of fingers inside herself, warming them up in her inner heat. That felt really good. Not the sexual sensations, just the thawing of her fingertips.

She brought the fingers back out and stroked her clit some more, thinking that would help with processing the burning sensation of the wind on her skin, but they immediately felt cold and numb again. More so now that they were wet. She didn't know what to do about the fingers on her other hand, so she tucked that hand under her armpit, but it only helped a little, so she switched hands and gave the other set of fingers a turn at hiding inside the warmth of her vagina. Every few seconds, she would switch again, alternately warming her fingertips.

After a few moments of this, her opening had stretched a bit and become more welcoming. Delia shoved her whole right hand inside her pussy, grinding it against her g-spot and gritting her teeth against the cold that threatened to freeze off her nipples. It felt really good in there. She wished she could crawl her whole body inside her warm pussy. Reluctantly, she pulled the hand out to insert the other hand.

The now-dripping right hand was immediately freezing, but the left sank into her warm hole with pleasure. She focused her mind on that sensation, ignoring the other. And then she had an idea. Lifting her butt up off the cold ground, she knelt. Then, she tucked a couple of her lubricated fingers into her ass hole. Only the tips went inside, and the cold, wet fingers were a shock at first, causing her to tighten that hole. But she could feel that it was just as warm inside there as in her vagina. It was another door to her inner warmth.

She'd practiced stretching her ass a bit, and she was determined to get the fingers of her left hand inside there before they froze off. She wiggled the lubrication from the fingertips around the first inch of her ass. It was drying quickly, though, in the frigid air. Again reluctantly, she pulled her other hand out of her pussy and rubbed its lubrication around on her ass hole. She started scooping as much of her secretions onto her fingers as possible, plunging them into her ass to get it wet. Then she tucked the right hand into her pussy, up to the wrist. Her body relaxed at the relief in her fingers, and she stuck two of the fingers of her left hand into her lubricated ass, all the way up to the knuckles.

Inside her ass, they also felt the relief of her internal body heat. She sighed, and then she shivered. She started moving the fingers in her ass, trying to stretch it open more, and wishing she would have tried harder at anal training. She didn't worry about whether anyone was watching; she was confident that they were all too focused on their own suffering and how to deal with it. She visualized stretching her ass wide open and getting her whole hand in there, like she had done with her pussy. It helped a little. She managed to get a third finger inside herself, but that was all she could manage. She knelt there on the ground, awkwardly folded to double penetrate herself, shivering violently. Delia was quite small compared to others in her circle, and at this moment, she truly envied the curvier initiates, who likely were generating more body heat than her small frame could muster.

Fingers snuggling inside her body, she heard boot beats down the trail. Another group of initiates was heading toward the clearing. As they came into view, she could see the black and red of their uniforms. It was a Dominant circle. They marched proudly up the trail and stopped when they came to the clearing full of submissive initiates, naked, touching themselves on the cold dirt. Most of the members of her circle stopped masturbating when they noticed the eyes of the Dominants on them. They turned their eyes away from the group of fully clothed initiates. Delia popped her fingers out of her ass but kept the other hand stuffed inside her warm cunt, sitting back on her heels and pressing her legs together as much as possible.

One of the young men in the other group laughed. "Look at how pathetic they are."

Delia felt a surge of heat, but it all went to her cheeks. She kept her eyes up, looking at the other group. Then she turned her face to Pehr, hoping for some kind of protection. The Instructor of Pain Processing made even, calm eye contact with her, and did nothing. That was when Delia realized that the instructor probably set up this accidental meeting of circles on purpose.

The instructor of the Dominants, however, did turn to the man who had laughed—the one with spiky, orange-red hair under his fur-lined, black hood—and he was frowning at him. "Submissives are not pathetic. They are precious gifts to us, and we must respect their unique skillset, not deride it."

The initiate with red hair crossed his arms over his chest. "I was practicing what I learned in Humiliation and Degradation, Master Caspius."

The man called Master Caspius was carrying a cane with him, and he stamped it against the ground. "Those skills are for use with one's own submissives, Initiate Gordaun. It is against our code of ethics to speak such a way to a submissive you have not collared or been granted use of."

The initiate that he chastised turned red in the face, but he kept his mouth pressed closed. Delia felt a sudden sense of affection for the man leading the initiates of dominance.

The woman next to her muttered. "Ugh, young Doms. I hope I find an experienced D-type when I graduate."

Until now, Delia had not given much thought to what age of Dominant she would prefer, but she found herself nodding in agreement as she eyed Master Caspius. She couldn't see much of the man in his winter gear. He wore black leather boots and black leather pants, and over it was a calf-length, fur-lined, black overcoat made of suede. His fingertips were covered in red leather gloves that peeked out the ends of his long sleeves. Rather than wool mitts, the Dominant and his initiates had thumb holes sewn into the long sleeves of their overcoats, so that only their fingertips poked out from the fur-lined warmth. In this way, they could tuck their fingers in away from the cold but still have full use of their hands when needed. Under his hood, the instructor had a trim, dark beard with a streak of gray right down the center, and she couldn't see much else of his face. She didn't care. She found herself fantasizing about following that calm, firm, authoritative voice.

"Five minutes is up," Pehr said, as though the other group were not even there at all. "Get your clothes on."

If the instructor had planned this diversion in the middle of their lesson, she had planned it well. In her embarrassment, under the gaze of the Dominant initiates, Delia had briefly forgotten about the fear of losing a toe from the cold. As she put her clothes back on as quickly as possible—socks first—she eyed Master Caspius and determined that she would find out what classes he taught.

CHAPTER TWO

Anal Training

Initiates at the College of Submission were encouraged to masturbate as often as they liked. As Instructor Pehr had said, it did help with some of their homework. Delia found the technique most useful when she had been taking Anal Training 101 last semester. Rubbing her clit helped her to focus on pleasure as she probed the tight, little hole. She had passed the class, but she had not explored the topic any further than was necessary to complete the homework and pass the tests. Poor Meela had been unable to bring herself to put in a butt plug in front of Instructor Lu and would have to take the class all over again over the summer.

Delia was currently putting Instructor Pehr's recommendation to use as she lay on her back in bed, knees tucked up near her chest, two fingers inserted in her ass. Meela looked over at her from her own bed in their shared dorm room.

"What are you doing?"

"Anal training."

"But you're not even taking that class right now."

"I developed an interest."

"Since when?"

"This morning."

"Are you kidding me? What could possibly have happened this morning that made you suddenly interested in anal training?"

"I realized it might become useful."

Meela's jaw dropped. "Are you telling me that what you learned from meditating for five minutes on not freezing your tits off was some epiphany that one day you may have to keep your fingers from frostbite inside your own ass hole? If that's the reason you're training, I think you should know that it's unlikely you'll need to—literally—pull that strategy out of your ass."

"Eh. Maybe you're right." She slid the fingers out of her butt hole. "I was only able to get two fingers in there just now anyway. That's even less than I fit in there this morning. I guess your body just kind of makes room when your brain tells it that it has to."

Delia jumped up to wash off her hands and throw her tunic back on. Thigh-high socks and tunics were the standard uniform for initiates in the College of Submission. They were simple and made dressing quick and easy. "Besides, I need to go visit the guidance counselor today."

"Why? It's the middle of the semester; you're not going to change classes, are you?"

Delia grinned. "I just want to plan ahead."

Without bothering to put on her cloak, she wrapped her shawl around her shoulders and put on a pair of gloves, and she was out the door. She walked briskly through the dormitory hallways and ran across campus to the administrative building where the guidance counselors kept their offices. It wasn't that late, but it was already dark out. When she got inside, she shivered away the cold and continued on to Counselor Nerva's office. She knocked at the door and didn't hear an answer.

She shifted her weight back and forth from one foot to the other, impatient. Maybe if Nerva wasn't there, she could just go in and peek at the class list to find out which ones Master Caspius taught. She bit her lip and reached for the knob.

"Delia?"

She jumped. Counselor Nerva was right behind her, holding a steaming mug. The counselor's wavy, ash-brown hair fell to just below her shoulders. She pushed up a pair of glasses on her nose as she spoke. "Did we have an appointment?"

"No, I just needed to talk to you. I want to get an early start at looking at my next set of classes."

The counselor shrugged. "I don't have any other appointments today. Come on in."

As soon as Nerva opened the door, Delia dashed inside and sat down in front of the desk, placing her hands in her lap and leaning forward.

Nerva laughed. "You seem eager."

She felt her face get hot. "No. I mean, yes. There are just some classes I want to take, and I want to make sure they don't get filled up."

Counselor Nerva sat down. "Sure. Which classes are you thinking about?"

Delia tapped her fingers against her lap. "Actually, I was impressed with Master Caspius's methods, and I was wondering what classes he will be teaching next semester."

Nerva raised an eyebrow. "Master Caspius teaches at the College of Dominance. He doesn't offer any classes that you can take."

She felt her shoulders droop. She'd thought that might be the case. "But some instructors cross-over and teach at both colleges. I thought I'd heard that Master Caspius had a course at the College of Submission?" She hadn't heard that, but it was worth a shot.

Counselor Nerva shook her head. "No, I'm afraid not. Master Caspius has never taught a cross-over course. He focuses solely on courses in Dominance." The counselor eyed Delia. Perhaps she could see the disappointment on her face. "Although..."

Delia lifted her chin and perked up at the sound of possibility in the counselor's voice.

"What courses are you currently taking? Let me pull open your file in my notebook." The counselor started rifling through pages as she spoke. "You see, Master Caspius is an Instructor of Anal Technique, and he does occasionally need a demo submissive to demonstrate the techniques in front of his initiates."

Delia hopped up onto her feet. "Really?"

Counselor Nerva looked up from her book with raised eyebrows. "Are you interested in applying for the demo position?"

"Absolutely."

Nerva crinkled her eyes. "Are you majoring in Anal Training?"

"No. I mean. Not currently, but I'm thinking about changing my major."

Nerva looked back down at the book. She had found Delia's file and was shaking her head. "I'm sorry. You've only taken Anal Training 101. The position is typically given to a student who's majoring in that specialty."

"But typically means not always, right?"

Counselor Nerva shook her head again. "Granting of the position is at the sole discretion of the instructor, but it's unlikely that Master Caspius will select a novice anal bottom."

"Okay, thanks, Counselor Nerva."

Delia turned and dashed out of the guidance counselor's office. Nerva followed her to the doorway.

"Wait. What about the other classes you're interested in?"

Delia called back over her shoulder. "I'll make an appointment another time."

The College of Dominance was way across campus. The two schools were separated as much as possible. Delia wished that she'd bothered to put on her cloak, but she wasn't going back to her dorm room for it. She'd just have to manage walking in the cold without a cloak. After all, she'd been wearing less this morning, and she survived. The cold was still biting, though, and her fingers got numb quickly with just the single layer of gloves.

Even moving briskly, it took her half an hour to get across campus. She'd never seen the main building at the College of Dominance up close before. It was foreboding. The structure climbed high, a castle made of dark gray stones, accented with red brick around the doorways and window frames. It made the windows look like red, angry eyes, and the main entrance, an open, yelling mouth. Still, it was just a building. She was cold, and her teeth were chattering, and she wanted to be inside.

She shoved through the door and looked around, and her body released a shiver at the relative warmth as the door closed behind her. The halls were empty at this hour, but they were not yet dark. Candles in sconces lighted the way brightly inside the ominous building, making it feel a touch more inviting. She exhaled in relief. If the lights were still lit, the instructors would likely be keeping office hours.

She took a first step forward and then realized that she didn't know where Master Caspius's office would be. Fortunately, like in the entrance at the College of Submission, a large map hung on the wall to her right, showing the layout of the building. Of course, the map didn't specify where particular instructors' offices were, but it at least showed her the general direction in which she should go. She started walking down the main hallway in the flickering candlelight. As she moved further down, she started to hear sounds of other people.

In fact, it sounded like a gathering of people was in a room up ahead. It must be some kind of common area. Delia was nervous at the prospect of talking to initiates of dominance, but she'd find the instructor's office much faster with some help. She kept close to the wall to her left, where the main hallway branched off into other hallways. As she got closer to the raucous, she heard a voice that sounded somewhat familiar. She hugged the wall, not wanting to be noticed too soon, and peered around the corner into the common area where some initiates were hanging out. She thought she'd recognized the voice. It was the guy with spiky red hair that she'd seen in the clearing. She certainly didn't want to ask him for help, nor did she especially like the idea of him knowing she was here. She ducked into one of the side hallways instead. She'd just have to find her own way to Master Caspius's office.

As she walked down this hall, which was not lit as brightly as the main one, she realized that without going past the common area to the main staircase, she'd be taking the long way around to the instructors' offices. Oh well, it was better than being stopped by that asshole initiate. She followed the hallway until it made an L-turn, and then she followed the new hallway down to its end. She looked around. There were a couple doors here, but she needed to go upstairs to the second floor, where the offices were. There were no obvious stairs.

She could hear the boot taps of someone else walking down a nearby hallway. She bit her lip. They might be able to help her, but she didn't know who might be coming this way. It could be the asshole initiate...or one of his asshole friends. She'd really prefer to get help from another instructor—someone she could trust. The footsteps were getting closer. She looked around at the doors again and saw that one was different from the others. She went for that one, clicking the door shut as softly as possible behind her. Or at least she tried to. The doors in the College of Dominance were heavy, and when she pulled it, it caught and then grated loudly as it closed.

She held her breath, knowing that whoever was in the hallway had heard the door. She looked around and saw that she was, in fact, in the stairwell. It wasn't lit in here, but some moonlight came in through a window, and she quickly went for the stairs. She sprinted all the way up to the next landing and panted, putting her hands on her knees to catch her breath. She hadn't heard anyone move the heavy door after her, and she laughed, realizing that no one knew she was here, and there was no reason for them to think it unusual that someone was using the stairwell.

She straightened up and shoved the door to the second floor open. If she remembered the map correctly, she'd come out near some administrative offices. The instructors' offices should be somewhere ahead. The lights in some of the hallways up here had already been put out. She hoped she wouldn't be too late to find Master Caspius. Forgetting about the pretense of stealth, she trotted down the hall. She felt relief when she heard another set of footsteps. She'd be able to ask one of the other instructors, or perhaps an administrative assistant, where to find the office she was looking for.

Except that's not who she found. She came to the junction at the end of the hallway and, as she turned toward the sound of boots, found herself face-to-face with Spiky Hair. He was grinning and had his arms crossed over his chest.

"I thought I saw you downstairs. You're the sub who had her whole hand inside her cunt at the clearing."

Delia felt her face get hot. She didn't know what to do, so she looked down at the floor. "Yes." There was no reason for her to lie. She knew what he had seen.

"What are you doing here, cunty? Feeling horny and thought you'd sneak in to find a Dom who could fill that needy hole?"

She looked up in alarm and shook her head. "No, I'm...just here on an errand." She stood up taller. "An instructor sent me."

The red-haired initiate looked at her. "Which instructor?"

"You wouldn't know them."

"Why do you think that? Do you think I'm stupid?"

"What? No."

"A pathetic little cunt submissive thinks that I'm too stupid to remember the name of an instructor?" Spiky Hair stepped closer, and Delia shrank back.

"It's not that. It's just that it was an instructor from the College of Submission, and—"

"Maybe the College of Submission is not doing a very good job of teaching its initiates to submit when they're clearly in the presence of a Dominant."

Delia felt her breathing speed up. She didn't know how to handle this situation, but she knew it wasn't right. The Dom initiate had continued stepping closer to her, until her back was up against the stone wall. He placed his hands to either side of her head, leaning in.

"If I had a crop right now, I'd smack you across the face with it."

Another voice spoke from behind him, soft, yet confident. "And then you would be expelled, Initiate Gordaun."

Gordaun's eyes widened, and he stood up, removing his hands from the wall. Delia looked around him and saw a large man with fully gray hair and a bushy, gray beard. The man did not seem to match the voice. He was hulking, and though his belly looked round under the tunic, he was clearly powerful.

Gordaun turned around. "Head Master Faust. I found this submissive lurking in our hallways."

"No rule against that," the older man said. "I'm going to review your curriculum, Initiate Gordaun. It seems there are some subtleties you are lacking. Now go on, and leave the submissive initiate to me."

The Dominant initiate quickly left the hallway, and Delia was left facing the intimidating figure who stood before her. The Head Master of the Dominants. A Dominant of Dominants. She blinked at him. She suddenly felt even smaller than usual. The Head Master took a deep breath and fixed her with a firm gaze.

"One thing about Dom initiates. Most of them don't know how to be quiet. Now, small one, I hear that you are on an errand?"

Under the frank gaze of the experienced Dom, Delia felt uncomfortable. She rubbed one ankle against the other and tried to make eye contact. "No, Sir. Not really. That's not exactly the case."

The Head Master put his hands on his hips. The gesture was not threatening, but it made him appear even larger. Delia shrank in her mind's eye.

"That's what I thought. What are you doing here, then? It's not exactly against the rules, but Initiate Gordaun is correct that it's frowned upon. And beside that, it can be dangerous for you, as you've seen. The Dominant initiates are not fully trained. Many do not know the boundaries of their power."

She nodded, feeling foolish for the first time since she'd devised this plan. "I really am here for a good reason, Sir. I'm applying for a demo position with Master Caspius."

The Head Master's eyes lit up. "Ah, you are a demo submissive? How exciting. Have you finished your application demonstration?"

She shook her head. "No, I was on my way to Master Caspius's office when I ran into...the initiate."

"Ah, well. Unfortunately, Master Caspius's office hours are over for the day."

Her heart sank. She couldn't believe she'd gone through all this trouble, and she wouldn't even get to speak to the instructor. Head Master Faust looked down at her, assessing her response.

"But, I'm actually on my way to have tea with him. Perhaps you'd like to join me, and you can make your application for the position?"

Delia felt her mouth stretch into a broad grin, and she nodded her head. She practically bounded down the hall as she followed the Head Master, ecstatic that she would accomplish her goal after all. She did wonder, however, what the application demonstration that Head Master Faust mentioned entailed.

CHAPTER THREE

A Demonstration

Sitting in the Head Master's office, on a chair facing the couch where both Head Master Faust and Master Caspius sat, Delia felt extremely small. Her feet dangled from the seat, not touching the floor. Master Caspius dwarfed her, and the Head Master of Dominance was even larger than him. Head Master Faust was a bear of a man with calm gray eyes that nearly matched his hair. Master Caspius, on the other hand, was like lightning. He was tall, though not unusually so, and where Head Master Faust was meaty muscle, Master Caspius was lean sinew. His face was long, and his chin narrowed almost to a point where the streak of gray ran down it. Master Caspius's eyes were like a roiling storm, sometimes appearing blue, sometimes gray, and at other times green. When Delia looked long enough, it seemed that his eyes were actually all of those colors at once.

And she could not help looking. She was drawn to this man's presence. He sat with his legs crossed in tight, black leather. In his lap, he held a saucer in one hand and the handle of a teacup in the other. The cane that he carried with him leaned against the couch next to his leg. It was a thin, black cane—clearly of use for swatting, not for aid in walking. He also wore a light blue tunic, tucked in, with laces at the chest. The laces hung loosely, undone, revealing a small patch of chest hair in the v-shaped opening.

Master Caspius set his teacup and saucer down on the small table between them and sat back on the couch. "So you'd like to apply for the demo sub position for Anal Techniques 231?"

Delia didn't realize the demo position was for an advanced class. She'd assumed it was for Anal Techniques 101. She nodded her head at him. "Yes, Sir."

"I assume you're majoring in Anal Training?"

She didn't want to stretch her lies too far. It would be too easy for the Dominant instructor to find her out. "No, Sir. I am not currently majoring in Anal Training."

"Minoring in it then?"

"No, but I'm confident that I can fulfill this role!"

"Have you at least taken some of the advanced courses in the field of study?"

Delia hesitated. She wanted to say yes, but again, she feared he would check her file.

"No, but I practice the subject on my own. As a hobby." That at least wasn't too far from a lie. And there was no way for him to check it out.

The Head Master's eyes twinkled as he watched the exchange. Master Caspius inhaled through his nose and nodded his head in thought. Abruptly, his head changed from nodding to shaking side to side. "No. No. I'm afraid you just won't do. I need a submissive with experience. It's an important part of the class I teach, and I get plenty of applicants from the major—submissives who take this field seriously."

"I do take it seriously! I was going to change my major; I just hadn't gotten around to it yet. I know I can do this for you."

"What is your current major, initiate?"

"Masochism."

Master Caspius's eyebrows rose, and he turned his mouth downward. "Hmm. Interesting, but not exactly the right skill set."

"Please, please, let me try."

Master Caspius sighed and uncrossed his legs. "Very well. I will allow you to proceed with an application demonstration, but I have little hope of you getting the position."

The two men stood, and the Head Master grasped Master

Caspius's hand. "Master Caspius, I'll allow you to borrow my office for the demonstration. Please lock up for me when you're done." The Head Master left the room, closing the door behind him, and leaving Delia alone with Master Caspius. She felt her heart flutter.

"Why isn't the Head Master staying?"

Master Caspius chuckled. "I imagine because he's not interested in girls."

She furrowed her brow. "Is that a joke about my size?"

"No. It's a statement of fact that Head Master Faust is gay."

She unfurrowed her brow. "Oh."

"All right then. Lean over the edge of the couch and pull up your tunic."

Delia's eyebrows shot up. "Uh, just like that?"

Master Caspius frowned. "Yes, if you're going to help me demonstrate anal techniques for my class, I'll have to test your ability to actually take a cock up the butt."

She started to panic. She'd just tested her abilities this morning, and she'd only fit two fingers in her ass. She took a deep breath and hoped that Master Caspius's dick wasn't too large. "Umm...may I see what I'm working with?"

"Of course."

The instructor unlaced his leather pants and folded them down over his hips, exposing himself to her. As soon as he did, she could smell the mild musk that had been held in by the leather. Her cunt responded to the scent immediately. That made her want to perform her task well even more. His cock looked fairly average, as she observed it. Maybe this wouldn't be so difficult.

Master Caspius grabbed a bottle off a shelf that hung over the couch. He poured the contents of the bottle over his hand and began rubbing the clear substance onto his cock. "I could also use a little assistance. Go ahead and lean over the edge of the couch, please."

Delia obeyed, standing at one side of the couch and bending at her hips, laying her torso across the armrest and her head and hands on the seat.

"The tunic."

She reached behind her and shimmied the loose fabric up over her rump, bunching it up around her waist.

"Yes, that's better. Spread your legs a bit."

She did. She couldn't help feeling her clit throb at the prospect of this powerful man eyeing her vulva and ass. Her heart was beating rapidly. Then, without warning, Master Caspius pressed his warm hand against her cunt, rubbing the flat of his palm over it and smearing her juices around. Part of his fingers rubbed over her clit as he did this, teasing it with light sensations. She sucked in a breath.

She tried to calm her breathing, and then she felt Master Caspius's dick press into her wet folds. He rubbed it in a downward motion, stroking his glans against her slippery clit. Already, it felt larger than it had looked, but mercy it felt so good against her.

"Spread your ass cheeks apart. Let me see what I'm working with, as well."

She reached behind herself, her face pressing into the couch cushion, and pulled her ass cheeks apart for inspection. She'd never been particularly shy. when it came to her body. As she stood there, she could hear the Instructor of Anal Technique continuing to rub the lubricant over his cock with a slick, fwapping sound.

Master Caspius grunted in what sounded like disapproval. "Doesn't look particularly well-trained to me. Masochist, indeed. Let's get on with it then. I'm ready."

Delia turned to look behind her, to see what size cock she'd promised to accept in her ass. Her body tensed up. Master Caspius's cock was thick. She'd never put anything that big in her butt during Anal Training 101. Not even anywhere near that big. She tried to keep the shock off her face, but she was never really that good at lying.

"Are you withdrawing your application, then?"

She narrowed her eyes at him. Nobody told Delia she couldn't do something. She was always the best. She always tried harder than any other initiate. "No, Sir."

"All right then."

If submissive initiates majoring in Anal Training could take Master Caspius's dick, then so could she. After all, her ass had accommodated three fingers this morning when she needed it to. It was simply mind over matter. She would fit Master Caspius's dick in her ass. She needed to. She had to get that demo position. It was the only way for her to spend more time with him. She knew her body wouldn't let her down.

Delia took a deep breath and tried to remember the techniques she'd learned in the 101 course, as well as the general calming techniques she'd learned from Instructor Pehr. She relaxed her body. And she felt the thick head of Master Caspius's dick press against her butt hole. It was slippery with lubricant, which he rubbed around her rim. He started to push the head against her ass hole.

She tensed again. "Aren't you going to warm me up with your fingers?"

Master Caspius answered sharply. "This is for Anal Techniques 231. Demo submissives for this course should be trained enough to accept a cock at any time. There should be no need for warmup."

Delia closed her mouth and focused on her breathing. She squeezed her eyes shut. Master Caspius's cock pressed against her again. There was a lot of resistance. Her butt was not opening up at all.

"Hmph."

Delia started to panic. She did not want to disappoint this Dominant. She didn't want to lose her shot before she'd even gotten it. She focused all of her effort on relaxing her body. She relaxed her eyes, keeping them closed. She relaxed her shoulders, softened her jaw, and unclenched her teeth. She let her body sink into the couch cushion and felt the arm of the couch press harder into her abdomen. She put her attention there, in the discomfort. It was a strategy she had learned. Focusing on one pain could take the mind off another. And she breathed. In. Out. Repeat.

Master Caspius continued to apply a steady, firm pressure to her ass hole, and slowly, that part of her body, too, relaxed. She felt the head of his dick pry her open. There was a bit of a burning sensation as it sank in.

"Are you done? Is this all you can take?"

"No, Sir. I'd like to continue my demonstration, please."

"Very well."

Master Caspius pressed his cock into her. It hardly moved with her tight sphincter wrapped around it. The lubricant seemed to be doing very little. Delia grasped desperately for some other technique that could help her. The pressure against her ass felt strange, and she involuntarily felt herself bearing down as though she were going to use the toilet. As she did so, however, miraculously, she felt the instructor's cock move a little further inside her. It was not comfortable, but it was going in. Remembering Instructor Pehr's lesson this morning, Delia moved one of her hands down between her legs and started rubbing her clit. Master Caspius pushed his cock into her again, and as he pushed, she bore down again with her anal muscles to allow his cock further entrance. The further in his cock went, the more it felt like his girth was stretching open her resistant hole. She rubbed her clit furiously, focusing on the pleasant sensations available to her. Focusing on the discomfort of her belly being pressed against the hard arm. Focusing on anything but the sensation of her ass hole feeling like it was being ripped open. She suddenly felt a strong burning feeling as Master Caspius pushed his cock inside her. But she also felt exultant. She'd gotten it in. She grinned and opened her eyes, turning her face back to look at the Dominant standing behind her.

"How did I do?"

Master Caspius pulled his dick out of her ass. The feeling of it passing back through her opening was intense. She gasped and clenched her ass hole closed as soon as he removed it.

"Little girl, you only took the first inch. I don't know why you came here to waste my time, but this is not the position for you."

Delia stood and turned around to see the instructor wiping off his cock on a small towel. Her tunic fell back down around her legs. Her shoulders slumped, and she tried to think of something to say. Her voice was quiet. "But I want to be your demo submissive..."

Master Caspius stopped wiping. "This is about an infatuation?" He sighed. "Stay out of the Dominants' area on campus. Go back to your dorm, little girl. I don't appreciate having my time wasted."

The instructor laced up his pants and opened the door for her. She walked out of the office numbly. But she had not given up yet. Delia went back to her dorm room that night, soaked her sore butt hole with a soothing tincture, and went to sleep with a plan.

CHAPTER FOUR

Help from a Friend

The next morning, Delia woke up before the bells. It was still dark out. This time of year, it was dark more often than it was light. She'd gotten used to it, though she'd never prefer it to the warm, long days of summer. The long darknesses were just another challenge to set her masochistic mind toward—they were a thing to endure and find some measure of enjoyment in.

As she turned her head to the side, she confirmed that Meela was still sleeping on the other side of the room. The submissive beds were not like the bed she'd had back at home. That bed had been large and comfortable. This was more like a plank, slightly wider than her body, that minimally raised her off the floor. It was not actually made of wood, but as hard as the mattress was, it might as well have been.

The good thing was it didn't creak when she rolled out of it, which she did now. She rolled into a crouch on the floor, looked once again at Meela, and then rose to her feet. She crept over to the dresser where her school supplies were kept, and she paused. The small dresser was another matter. It was made entirely of raw, unstained wood, and it always made noise when she opened and closed it. There were no metal sliding mechanisms like well-made drawers had. No, these were made to remind the submissive initiates of their place here.

Delia drew in a breath and pulled on the drawer—slowly. It came out an inch and got stuck. Of course it did. She gritted her teeth and gave it a tug, and the rough wood popped and then ground together, making a squeak and then a scraping sound. She gritted her teeth together harder and growled under her breath. She glanced over her shoulder at Meela. Her friend didn't seem to have heard anything. That was a miracle. Meela was the lightest sleeper Delia had ever met. The slightest sound in the night would wake her.

She let out her held breath and turned back to the dresser. She just needed to pull it open a little more. The things never opened smoothly. She shimmied the drawer back and forth, causing the items inside to clink together, coaxing it open further. There. She looked into the drawer. It was too dark to make out the contents, but there wasn't much in there. She put both hands inside the drawer and felt around.

Her fingers brushed against a few small, smooth objects, but there were only a couple of items in there of the shape she was looking for—thick, flat, and rectangular. Her hands found each of them. One was a textbook with a rough cover. The other's surface was similar. It was a box made of unfinished wood, much like the dresser in which it was kept. The two objects felt similar, but she knew which was the textbook when she felt around the edges and her fingers brushed the telltale ridges of pages. She removed her right hand from the book and brought it over to the box, carefully lifting it from the darkness.

There was a singular window in the dorm room, in the far wall between the two sleeping areas. Moonlight shone in from it, falling across the floor. Delia crept back over to her bed and squatted down onto the edge of the mattress, placing the wooden box in the streak of moonlight on the floor in front of her. She undid the little metal latch and lifted the lid. Inside, the box was lined with green felt, and in a neat little row, from smallest to largest, lay her set of anal training plugs.

They were a nice set, made of polished, stainless steel. Moonlight glinted off the metal, and in the corner of the box, snugged above the smallest butt plug, was a round, flat, metal canister, much like one might keep lip balm in. She lifted the canister from the box and twisted the lid open. There was still plenty of lubricant inside. She set the open canister next to her on the bed and lifted the smallest plug from its groove in the felt. Where she lifted it, a cutout in the wood, just the right size for the plug, was left behind. Each plug had such a holder to keep them from shifting around inside the box.

Delia looked down at the small plug in her hand. She unwrapped her fingers, leaving the butt plug lying on her flat palm. It was weighty, despite its diminutive size. She wrapped her fingers back around it, feeling the cool metal against her skin, and nodded to herself. Then she pulled her nightshirt up and off over her head and spread her knees open. She let her ass hang off the edge of the low mattress, and she dipped a couple fingers into the thick lubricant. As she rubbed it around onto the steel plug, it liquified from the warmth of her hand. She wiped the remaining lubricating balm onto the exterior rim of her butt hole. Then she took a deep breath, let it out, and pressed the tapered, not quite pointy, tip of steel against her closed hole.

With the lubricant and the tiny, tapered end, the tip of plug inserted easily. She held it there, just the tip inside her, trying to get her head in the right place. She thought about Master Caspius's earthy, stormy eyes and applied pressure to the plug. It slipped halfway in quite easily. It was only a one-inch diameter, after all. Still, she did not have the plug all the way in yet. She pulled it most of the way back out and then pressed it to the halfway point again, just below the thickest part of the plug. She repeated this motion several times, getting the lubricant spread around inside her. As she made the tiny thrusts at the very interior of her ass, she imagined Master Caspius's cock pressing into her once again.

She applied firm, steady pressure to the plug, much like the Dominant instructor had done with his cock. Not forcing it in. Just pressing, pressing until her tight muscle gave way. And it did. The plug popped into her ass hole, suddenly sliding all the way in. She felt her hole clench closed around the narrow handle at the end of the plug. It was such an intense sensation, getting something into her ass. It wasn't unpleasant, but it felt strange and different. Almost like a sense of relief. It was like the feeling you get when you stretch a particularly tight muscle past its point of familiar and comfortably stretching, and after about fifteen seconds or so, the muscle gives way.

The small plug really wasn't that hard to get in. It was mostly for getting used to the sensation of having something in one's ass, or for getting warmed up for bigger insertions. Even the least trained submissives had gotten the hang of it in class. Delia took a breath and exhaled as she pulled the plug back out. Her untrained ass was quite sensitive, and she once again had that brief, intense sensation of tight muscles giving way involuntarily.

As she looked around, she realized she hadn't prepared any towels for laying the used butt plugs on. Instead, she laid the now-warm metal on top of her crumpled nightshirt. It would get washed anyway. Then she moved her hand to the next plug in the box. This one was a one-and-a-half-inch diameter. Just large enough to pose a bit of a challenge to the anal novice.

It had taken her some time last semester, but Delia had been able to train herself to take the second smallest butt plug. Tonight, however, she didn't have time for working her way up to it. She was determined to get it in and move on to the larger training toys.

As with the smallest plug, Delia smeared some of the melting lubricant onto this one. It shouldn't be too hard to get in with the lube from the first plug making the way ready for this one. She cleared her mind, practicing the breathing techniques she had learned from Instructor Pehr. Anal training wasn't so different from masochism training; she didn't understand why everyone thought she couldn't do this.

That thought fueled her desire to get the second plug in. She'd show them. She didn't need to be majoring in Anal Training to be the best demo submissive Master Caspius had ever used. She plunged the one-and-a-half-diameter plug into her slippery ass hole. The taper made it slide in easily, but it stopped firmly just before she had half the plug inside her. It didn't hurt at this level of stretching; it was just the point at which the plug naturally reached resistance.

As with the first, she began thrusting the butt plug in and out of her hole, trying to loosen it up and relax the muscle. She swirled the plug around and pushed it from side to side, urging her muscle to loosen. And she pressed, steadily she pressed, willing her body to accept the larger object. It refused. But she continued. She was not going back to sleep tonight until she got this plug in.

She pulled it out and applied more lubricant. She gritted her teeth and pressed. The plug would not go in more than halfway.

"Oh, for goodness sake! You have to stop fighting it!" Meela jumped up off her mattress. The plug shot out of Delia's ass and onto the hardwood floor.

"Meela. You're awake."

"Of course I'm awake! You think I haven't heard you over there grunting for the past half hour?"

"Sorry I woke you up."

"Forget about it. I don't know why you're suddenly insisting on learning how to stretch your ass, but I know you. Once you set your mind to something, you don't let it go. And I am not going to spend the next month not getting any sleep. So just let me help you."

Delia chuckled. "I appreciate the offer, but you didn't even pass Anal Training 101."

Meela's face turned red and she looked at the floor, clenching her fists. "I know..." Delia's friend shifted her gaze to look down into Delia's eyes. Her voice got small. "But it's not because I wasn't good at it...I just hate having an audience."

That made sense. Her shyness had always been Meela's downfall. Maybe her friend could help her. It was worth a shot.

"Okay. What do you suggest I do, then?"

"First of all, you've got to stop treating the smaller plugs like they are a challenge."

"Pfft! In case you haven't noticed, they are a challenge."

"They're not, and you've got to quit telling yourself that."

Delia closed her mouth. Hearing shy, quiet Meela sound so confident about this was weird.

Meela continued talking. "Not only are the small plugs not a challenge, but none of the plugs should ever be unpleasant."

"That's stupid. Of course it's unpleasant!"

"Only because you've convinced yourself that it is. Delia, you're always trying to make everything so difficult for yourself. Whenever the hard way is available, you choose it. It's like you can't convince yourself that you've done a good enough job unless you struggle. You're set on tackling every problem in exactly the same way—like a challenge that makes you into some kind of martyr. Let me tell you something. Not everything has to be a battle. Not every task requires Instructor Pehr's methods. In fact, forget all about pain processing for now. Anal play should never require pain processing."

"And what do you suggest I try instead?"

"All you need is Instructor Kondari's methods."

"Mindfulness? You think I'm going to stretch open my ass by paying more attention to how it feels?"

Meela just looked at her and nodded.

Okay, now Meela was talking nonsense. Delia looked up at her friend, letting her continue her ridiculous explanation.

"When you get to the point where one of the plugs is an actual challenge for you, the challenge should not be painful or something you're trying to avoid. It should be something you're looking forward to, like when you get better at a game and can suddenly play at a higher skill level."

"You're just repeating that philosophy stuff Instructor Kondari talks about. It doesn't mean that you could do any better at this than I can."

Meela narrowed her eyes. "Oh yeah?"

Delia's friend snatched the largest plug from the open box between them. She didn't even ask to borrow the lubricant. She just spit on the giant ball of metal, rubbed her spit around, and squatted on the floor in front of Delia. Then, Meela pressed the massive plug between her ass cheeks, pumping it into herself a few times before pressing the plug up into her rectum. It disappeared inside her, save for the handle at the end.

Delia's mouth hung open. "How did you do that?"

Meela shrugged. "Studying philosophy and listening to my body."

That sounded a little woo-woo to Delia, but clearly there was something Meela was doing that worked. "Can you teach me?"

Suddenly, Meela reverted to her usual demeanor. She looked down at the floor and rubbed her cheek with her knuckle. "I don't know. There's not much to teach. Like I said, I just followed Kondari's mindfulness techniques."

Delia threw her hands up in frustration. "That's all you can tell me?"

"Well...I mean...maybe I can guide you along the way."

"Okay, let's start with you telling me how focusing on the pain is going to make this process easier."

"You're not going to focus on the pain."

"So it's an attention-shifting exercise. To be mindful about other things while ignoring what's happening to my ass. I can do that, but it would be a lot easier if I wasn't the one inserting the plugs."

Meela sighed and shook her head. "You're not going to divert your attention elsewhere. The mindfulness should be focused on your own body."

Delia stared at her friend blankly.

Meela sighed again. "You're not going to be focusing on pain because you are going to focus on pleasure!"

"You mean rubbing my clit?"

"Well, yes, that can be part of it, too. But I was speaking specifically about the pleasure involved in anal stimulation."

Delia furrowed her brow. "Wait a minute. Are you saying that taking anal is so easy for you because you like it?"

Meela's face flared red. She covered it with her hands and nodded.

"But we're submissives. We're supposed to endure for others; we're not supposed to do things for our own pleasure."

"Who ever told you that? Serving can be a pleasure." Meela kept her eyes down. "And sometimes...the things we do to serve others are also pleasurable to us in their own right." Meela raised her chin and looked into Delia's eyes.

Delia felt her mind processing this information. She did get enjoyment out of submitting, but it was almost always a mental satisfaction. The tasks she did were not pleasurable in their own right. They were challenging, and she loved the challenge. She loved doing better than someone else. She loved the praise she got after a job well done. In truth, she was a validation slut. She wanted to do well. And she wanted someone to notice.

She was, however, curious about Meela's hypothesis. "Explain to me how anal play is pleasurable."

Meela's eyes seemed to glaze over as she thought about it, like she was imagining a scene in her head. "Surely you must have felt something when you were inserting the plugs. There are...many, many nerves in the anal region."

"Yes, the feeling was very intense."

Meela's eyes brightened and came back to the present. "Yes, exactly! That feeling of intensity, that is the nerve-endings in your rectum."

"Can we not use the word rectum? It's not very sexy."

Meela shrugged, ignoring the comment. "That feeling is the one you want to focus on when you are training. But when you're new to it, you can't overdo it. You've got to pay attention to when you first have sensations in those nerves. When it happens, stop there, pay attention to it, enjoy it right there in that moment."

Delia groaned. "This method is going to take forever. I don't have all semester. I need to learn to be able to do what you do."

Meela shook her head. "This is the only way I know how to do it."

"Okay, well, how long did it take you to get to that point?"

"Me? Oh, I don't know. I wasn't really counting the days...Probably about a month. Maybe a little less than that."

"A month? Hmm...that's not that long, but I'm going to need to be ready faster than that."

"Ready for what? Why is this so important to you?"

Delia stood up from the bed and faced her friend. "Okay, listen. There is a position open for a demo anal submissive. I want that position, and I will do anything to get it."

Meela looked at her like she was doing something absolutely stupid. "Why?"

"I just do, okay?"

"You don't have to be the best at everything, you know. You're going to get a position when we graduate. Is that what you're worried about?"

Delia startled. "What? No. I'm not worried that I won't get a position. Why would you say that?"

Her friend looked at her, concerned. "I just don't understand why you're doing this."

"I told you why. I want the demo position. You said you would help me."

Meela shook her head. "Yeah, I'll help you. I can see you're not going to let this go, and I don't want to go all semester without any sleep while you stay up fighting with your anus like it's a freaking peg hole that needs to be drilled."

Delia grinned. "Well it is, isn't it?"

"Shut up."

"Also, anus is not a sexy word, either."

"You are going to drive me insane no matter what, aren't you? Let's get ready for breakfast, and we can start practicing during lunch. I want to get this over quickly as much as you do."

CHAPTER FIVE

Learning about Pleasure

"See? That's about as far as I got earlier this morning."

Delia lay on her back across the shorter length of her mattress, with her feet raised off the floor, knees bent and spread open. Meela kneeled in front of her, watching.

Meela put a hand to her chin and nodded. "Hmm...That's actually pretty good. Once you've gotten the number two plug in, I have some other methods we can work with."

"Like what?"

"I don't want to intimidate you. Let's take this one step at a time. Now that I've seen what you can do, let me help you find the right mindset."

"Okay, yeah, let's get this plug in there!"

Meela giggled. "Not yet. First, we're going to have a lesson on pleasure."

Delia raised up on her elbows and looked at her friend skeptically.

"Hey, you asked for my help. Are you going to trust me, or not?"

Delia sighed and flopped her head back down onto the pillow behind her, closing her eyes. "You're my only hope. Show me your way."

"Okay, keep your legs just like they are."

Delia could hear Meela get up and walk across the room. When she came back, she said, "Lift your hips up off the mattress."

She complied, and Meela stuffed another pillow under Delia's bottom. She felt even more exposed to her friend. It was a little strange. It almost felt like Meela was topping her. Her pussy was getting wet at that thought.

She heard what sounded like a sigh come out of Meela's mouth, only her friend had gotten really close to her. The warm breath of the sigh cast itself across her labia, comforting and relaxing.

Delia opened her eyes and looked down at Meela kneeling between her legs. "What are you doing?"

"Teaching you about pleasure. Close your eyes."

She did close her eyes, but she kept talking. "I know about pleasure, Meela. It's not like I never masturbate."

Meela shook her head between Delia's legs, and Delia felt the dark, soft hair of Meela's head caress her thighs as she did. "Even when you masturbate, it's about competition. Remember when you spent months trying to get yourself to squirt? You masturbated constantly, but I wouldn't say you were enjoying yourself through all of it."

Delia frowned. "Do you have to bring that up right now?" Squirting was the one thing she had tried that she just couldn't get her body to cooperate with. It made her irritable to be talking about her failure while she was trying to accomplish a new achievement.

Meela cocked her head and raised her eyebrows. "Fine. But there is nothing for you to accomplish in this task. Come if you want. Don't come if you want. Come once. Come a hundred times. I have a goal in mind, and I'm not going to tell you what it is. There's no way for you to win."

"Fuck you!"

Meela grinned. "Oh, you wish." Then those full lips and gorgeous gray-green eyes dropped into Delia's cunt, and suddenly Meela's mouth was pressed into her labia, and her friend's tongue began slowly lapping at her clit.

She sucked in a breath and pushed her cunt into Meela's face, raising her hips a little higher. Meela lapped faster at her clit, straight up and down, like a cat lapping up milk.

Delia groaned. "Am I supposed to come or not?"

Meela raised her mouth. "I don't know. What do you want to do?" She didn't let Delia answer before pressing her mouth back into Delia's cunt, circling her tongue around her clit.

Delia moaned and arched her back. Meela withdrew her tongue and pressed her lips around Delia's clit, sucking at it. Then the other woman stuck her tongue out, gently flicking it at her inner labia, tracing the edge of one of them with her tongue, down to the opening of her pussy. Meela slowly stuck her warm tongue into her wet opening, pressing it in and just holding it there. Delia couldn't take the lack of stimulation when her friend's tongue was right there. She thrust her hips up in small movements, forcing Meela's tongue inside her. Meela grabbed her by the ass and plunged her tongue inside, fucking her with her tongue.

Abruptly, Meela stopped, pulling her mouth away, hands still grabbing each of Delia's ass cheeks. Meela grinned. "Oh, did you want something? There was something that you liked?"

"You bitch."

"Be nice, Delia. Be a good little submissive."

Meela plunged her mouth back into her cunt, licking at her clit, flicking her tongue against it, first back and forth and then side to side. Her friend lifted her dark, wavy-haired head, meeting Delia's eyes as she inserted two fingers into her slick pussy. Meela immediately found the raised, engorged area of her g-spot and started massaging it with her two fingertips. Delia felt herself close to coming. Meela massaged faster.

Then she stopped. "Eh. I can't tell if you like this much."

"I like it."

"Well, then maybe I should stop. You are a masochist after all. You take a lot of pride in that. I bet orgasm denial is totally your thing. You probably enjoy feeling all pent up and angry."

"I thought you were supposed to be teaching me about pleasure."

"Nah, you get your pleasure from pain. You're probably even hoping you'll fail at getting the demo position so you can suffer. I bet that's your real plan."

Delia was about to retort, but Meela pressed her mouth back against her clit, and instead she let out a moan and pressed her hips toward Meela's face. Then Meela lowered her mouth and started lapping up the fluids that had built up around the opening of her cunt.

Meela lifted her mouth. "I think I'll ruin your plan."

The beautiful woman who Delia shared a dorm room with slid her tongue around the edge of her pussy's opening, and then she kept running her tongue further down, reaching the rim of Delia's ass hole. Meela reached up and put her fingers back inside of Delia's pussy, massaging her engorged g-spot once again. Meela also began to run her tongue around the outside edge of her ass hole.

Delia felt so ready to come that she would have let Meela do anything to her right now. The normally shy woman flicked her tongue at Delia's ass hole before plunging it inside. She gasped. She'd never had a tongue inside her ass before. She couldn't believe Meela was doing this. And at the same time, Meela was plunging her two fingers in and out of Delia's pussy. Her friend got into a rhythm, fucking her pussy with her fingers and her ass with her tongue, both holes being plunged into at the same time. The tongue in her ass increased the sensation of wanting to come from Meela's fingers rubbing against her g-spot. She was so close.

Then Meela stopped again and raised her head, giving her a mischievous look.

"Why are you stopping?"

"I just wanted to see your face."

Slowly—so slowly—Meela pulled the two fingers out of Delia's cunt.

"No, no, don't stop."

"Oh, I'm not stopping."

Meela pressed her tongue into Delia's clit and used her whole head to rock her tongue back and forth across it. As she did, she pressed the tips of those fingers, wet with pussy juices, up against Delia's slobbery ass hole.

Meela lifted her head. Delia still hadn't gotten to come. Her friend kept stopping. "Should I stop?" Meela asked.

"No, don't stop. Don't stop."

"Okay."

Meela pressed her tongue back against Delia's clit and pushed her fingers inside, penetrating Delia's ass. Delia gasped, and Meela kept licking at her clit in a steady rhythm, rocking her head. Delia could feel Meela's chin rubbing around in her fluids, adding extra sensation as she ate her out with her whole face. At the same time, Meela's fingers gently massaged the inside of Delia's ass. The fingers were all the way inside her, and Meela butted the knuckles of her hand up against the outside rim of Delia's ass hole as she made tiny thrusts inside her, not pulling the fingers out much with the backward motion. It felt like an internal massage, and it felt great.

Delia's orgasm burst forth, and she grabbed her friend's head, keeping Meela's tongue against her clit as she thrust her hips upward into her friend's face. As she came, she could feel her ass hole clenching against Meela's fingers, and Meela kept thrusting into her ass as her clit throbbed into her friend's mouth.

When she was done, Meela gently withdrew the fingers. "Now. Tell me about the pain processing techniques you employed while I fingered your ass."

Delia narrowed her eyes at Meela. "You know I didn't use any."

"Is that so? Hm. Interesting."

"Yeah, but it was just a couple fingers. That was nothing."

"That's true." Meela looked out the window just as a bell started ringing. "I've got to get to class. We'll practice again tonight."

Delia stood up. She had a class to get to, as well. "Okay." She felt a little disappointed. They hadn't really made much progress. After all, two fingers was only about the same girth as the smallest butt plug in her set. As Meela wrapped herself in a cloak and left the room, Delia wiped herself off with a towel and put her tunic back down over her ass. Her next class was Obedience Practices, and Instructor Lau'Ronya had a way of making students want to show up on time.

CHAPTER SIX

Respect Your Dominant

Instructor Lau'Ronya paced at the front of the class. She was a fairly energetic, middle-aged woman. She was plump, and most of the weight seemed to go to her breasts, which protruded under her teaching robe. The Instructor of Obedience's hair was blonde and cut into a straight bob with bangs. On most people, it would have been an aging, or even severe, look, but for Instructor Lau'Ronya, it somehow made her look childlike, with her bright blue eyes and round, chubby face peeking out from under the fringe of blonde.

When Delia signed up for the class on Obedience Practices, she was really expecting a different kind of teacher. She had assumed that anyone teaching obedience must be a real bore. She had imagined someone standing stock-still at the front of the class, reciting methods in a monotone. Instructor Lau'Ronya was not like that. She was a vibrant, happy woman. Perhaps one of the happiest people Delia had ever met. And Instructor Lau'Ronya credited all her happiness to her skills in obedience.

At the moment, she was discussing one of her six patented obedience skills. The class was supposed to learn and practice all six before the semester was through. They were currently on number two: respect your Dominant. Instructor Lau'Ronya had called the first skill—self-maintenance—the most important of all the skills. Delia didn't see how that could possibly be. After all, she was also taking a course this semester on Selflessness, which seemed to be the exact opposite of paying attention to one's own needs. Still, the obedience instructor had insisted that they spend several weeks on the practice of self-maintenance alone.

Even if she didn't quite understand the importance, self-maintenance had been fairly easy to grasp. She'd thought what it meant to respect one's Dominant, on the other hand, would have been self-evident, but she was definitely learning things she had not known. For instance, she was learning that respecting one's Dominant meant, in part, not just listening to the Dominant's commands and accepting their punishments, but also holding oneself accountable for feelings about one's Dominant. She did not consider that she would ever have to take responsibility for ensuring she had good feelings for her Dominant. After all, wouldn't that be their responsibility?

But no. According to Instructor Lau'Ronya, it was the submissive's responsibility to practice gratitude for one's Dominant.

"Sometimes your Dominant will do things that you do not like. Sometimes, they will even do things that make you question whether you have submitted yourself to the wrong person. I know it's hard to believe right now, when you are young and uncollared. You dream of a Dominant sweeping you off your feet and giving you the most fulfilling life you could imagine. Being disenchanted with your Dominant probably seems impossible. But I am telling you that it can, and probably will, happen at some point. And when that happens, here is exactly what you will need to do: recite gratitudes.

"If all you can see are your Dom's shortcomings, that is a failing of yours, not of theirs. It means you are choosing to focus on the negative. And the only way to remain happy and obedient is to focus on the positives—on your Dominant's strengths. After all, you wouldn't want anyone judging you solely on your weaknesses, would you? Every day, starting the first day of your submission, you should recite to yourself three things you are grateful for about your Dominant."

There were some murmurings among the students, and one woman raised her hand. "Yes?" Instructor Lau'Ronya asked.

"What if your Dominant is not doing anything wrong per se, but they aren't utilizing you to your full potential?"

"Ah, a common fear, especially during the early days of sub

frenzy. In that case, you should also practice your gratitudes. It will remind you of all the times that your Dominant is making use of you. But also, I will give you all some advice—a warning, if you will— never tell your Dominant how you can serve. It is their responsibility to choose what tasks you are worthy of, and when you perform tasks that have not been asked of you directly, you are disrespecting your Dominant. It is not your place to make use of your skills; it is your place to be useful. If you negotiated an appropriate match, you will be used in the ways appropriate to your service."

"But what if we're bored?"

"Then return to skill one, self-maintenance. Never, ever, bother your Dom with the complaint that you are bored. There is almost nothing more disrespectful." Instructor Lau'Ronya leaned in. "And here's the real secret. The more respectful you are of your Dominant, the more they will be interested in discovering what uses you can serve. Complaining is just a lazy way of expressing what you want. You always end up happier when you avoid complaining."

Another teacher entered the room, and the obedience instructor popped back up to a standing position. Delia recognized the other instructor right away by his snug leather pants, the solitary streak of gray down the center of his beard, and of course, the black cane he carried in with him. Even from here, she could see the storm roiling in his multicolored eyes.

The bubbly submissive instructor smiled and gestured to the man next to her with a hand. "Now, let's talk about how the skill of always remaining respectful applies to your Dominant's sexual needs. I've brought in Master Caspius from the College of Dominance to help me demonstrate. Who would like to go through an example scenario with him? I'll leave the selection to Master Caspius."

Delia nearly jumped out of her chair as she raised her arm, straining it as high into the air as she possibly could. Damn her short stature. She was in the middle of the rows of students, and she wasn't sure if Master Caspius would see her. She waved her arm around, and the Master of Anal Techniques made brief eye contact with her before dismissing her as an option. She still kept her arm in the air until he made his selection, pointing out a woman near the front who had a long braid with the sides of her head shaved. Delia slumped back into her seat and watched the lucky bitch go to the front of the class.

As the submissive initiate stood next to him, Master Caspius leaned over and placed his cane against the side of the desk at the front of the room. "Remove your tunic," the Dominant instructor said to his volunteer.

The woman pulled off her top and stood naked in her socks and boots. She was a heavy woman of medium height. She had a large, soft belly and large, soft hips. Her breasts were an average size. Her bush was dark and full and trimmed up the sides, almost like it matched the shaved sides on her head.

"Lean over the desk, please," Master Caspius said.

The woman with the shaved sides leaned over the instructor's desk.

"I'd like to fuck you in the ass," Master Caspius said.

The woman stood upright. "I'm not prepared for that."

And that's where Instructor Lau'Ronya jumped in. "Wrong! You've just disrespected your Dominant. Let's try again."

"Lean over the desk, please," Master Caspius said.

The woman complied.

"I'd like to fuck you in the ass," Master Caspius said.

The woman said nothing, though her body appeared to tremble on top of the desk. Instructor Lau'Ronya turned to the class, explaining the scenario. "Although Mereth is not disobeying her Dominant's request, her body language is still expressing that she does not trust him. Trust is an essential aspect of respect."

The woman on the desk tried to still her shaking. Master Caspius pulled a small container out of a pouch at his side. He opened it and dipped his fingers in. Delia leaned forward at her desk, watching intently. Then Master Caspius pressed his fingers between the woman's cheeks, prepping her with lubricant. As the class watched, he pressed his thumb into her ass hole, massaging it. The female submissive moaned, her cheek smushed into the desktop. Then Master Caspius put in two fingers, working her rim, helping it to open up.

Instructor Lau'Ronya addressed the student leaned over the desk. "Very good, Mereth! You may stand and put your tunic back on." She turned to address the class. "You see, first of all, Master Caspius said that he would like to fuck her ass; he did not say he would do so currently. Respect requires listening. Second of all, as an educated

Dominant, Master Caspius knows how to tell on his own whether a submissive is ready for a particular sex act. Respect requires trust. You must trust that your Dominant is intelligent and making the right choice. Had Master Caspius decided to continue with anal sex after some stretching, it would be the submissive's job to accept that decision as well, knowing that the Dominant always has the relationship's best interest at heart."

Delia thought about the Dominant initiate, Gordaun. "What if the Dominant doesn't actually have the relationship's best interest at heart? What if they do something that puts their submissive in unnecessary danger?"

Instructor Lau'Ronya put her hand to her chin, as though she were considering. "It is important for a submissive to distinguish between being put in pain and being put in actual harm. If you are in actual harm, there are, of course, processes for removing yourself from service. No submissive is ever required to serve a Master they cannot respect. I would caution, however, that if you choose to disobey your Dominant's order—and you do not wish to leave their service—you may find yourself involuntarily uncollared. Always consider your actions, and practice respect any time you wish to remain in service. The vast majority of Dominants want to keep their submissives happy. After all, happy submissives serve better." Instructor Lau'Ronya smiled like a kid showing off a prized piece of their rock collection.

The instructor turned to the Dominant instructor beside her. "Now, Master Caspius, I believe you had a bonus lesson you would like to present to the submissives here."

Delia perked up in her seat, leaning forward again.

"Yes, I want to talk to you all about another aspect of respect." Delia slumped down. She thought Master Caspius was going to talk to them about anal techniques.

"In the example scenario, I told the submissive what I wanted, but sometimes, your Dominant may ask you what you want or what you prefer. When that happens, you should always answer honestly. Many submissives have an inclination to answer with what they think their Dominant wants to hear from them. This is lying, and it is a serious form of disrespect." Master Caspius locked eyes with Delia as he said this. She pursed her lips together and looked down at her desktop, slumping further down to avoid any other eyes on her.

The Instructor of Anal Techniques returned his attention to surveying the rest of the class. "If your Dominant, for instance, asks you if you want them to fuck you in the ass, and you don't, then you should say so. They are asking you for your preference in that matter. Always be attentive to whether your Dominant is stating their own desires or asking you about yours."

Instructor Lau'Ronya bounced on her toes and beamed at Master Caspius. "A very good point! Thank you!"

"My pleasure, Instructor Lau'Ronya." Master Caspius gave a small nod of the head to the Instructor of Obedience, picked up his black cane, and strolled out of the room. Delia kept her head down, but she still followed him with her eyes.

Instructor Lau'Ronya went on to talk about more examples of how respect plays out in Dominant-submissive relationships, but Delia couldn't focus. Her mind kept going back to thinking about Master Caspius's statement and the question she had no answer to: what if your preference is to do whatever your Dominant wants? What if you have no desire of your own, other than to serve? What if finding out what they want from you and doing whatever it takes to make that happen is your desire?

She needed to get back to her dorm room and find out the next step from Meela.

CHAPTER SEVEN

Making a Mess

Delia was pretty sure she failed at any attempt of selflessness during Selflessness class, her final class of the day. She spent the whole time thinking about when she'd get out of there so she could practice her anal training. That and thinking about how she'd show Master Caspius for underestimating her. She kind of regretted it now because she realized that Instructor Pratom's class was probably the one she would most benefit from this semester. Embodying selflessness, according to the instructor, helped a submissive become efficient and hard working. That was exactly what Delia wanted to be.

Oh well, she would practice her work ethic by putting everything into her training session with Meela, who now sat behind her, naked but for her socks, stroking Delia's clit while Delia, herself, pushed the lubed up, one-and-a-half-inch steel plug into her ass. With some small resistance, it went in.

"Yay! You did it." Meela stopped masturbating Delia's clit to reach her arms around Delia's waist and clap her hands. "Now, pull the plug partway out and then back in again."

Delia held the handle of the butt plug and gave it a firm, slow pull, feeling her ass open up again for the widest segment of the plug. When she stopped pulling, her ass sucked the plug right back in.

Meela stood over her, watching. "Good. Keep doing that. Like it's a really short dildo that you're fucking yourself with."

Delia pulled the plug out of her still-tight ass hole, watching her body suck it back in each time. It did kind of turn her on to watch her hole open up around the toy and then slurp it back in. She felt herself getting wetter, and she sped up the motion of pulling on the inserted butt plug. Every time the plug went back in, she felt a delicious sensation in the nerves around her hole. It surprised her every time.

When she looked back up to grin at Meela over her progress, she saw that her friend was now wearing a harness around her hips. The harness held a dildo pressed firmly against her dark mound of pubic hair.

"What's that for?"

"Plugs can only do so much of the work of training. You'll need to be able to handle depth, as well, and plugs just don't do a good job of that. They're for girth. Go ahead and turn around, and let me see how you're doing with the plug. On your hands and knees."

The dildo had not looked large—it was quite small, in fact—so Delia was not worried...too much. As she kneeled on her hands and knees, Meela leaned over behind her and tugged at the plug in her ass. "Hmm. That looks pretty good." Her friend pulled the plug partway out and let it slink back into Delia's ass. "Nice."

Meela knelt down behind Delia and put her hands on Delia's hips. Delia waited, anticipating the moment that her friend would take the plug out and replace it with the dildo. But she didn't. Instead, Meela rubbed the head of the fake cock in the slippery valley between her labia and pressed the dildo into Delia's cunt, immediately starting to fuck her. Delia moaned and felt a small gush of fluid from her cunt. She suddenly felt so full, despite the small size of the dildo. She had a toy in both her cunt and her ass, and she could feel the dildo inside her pushing against the butt plug through her inner wall and moving it around. The effect was exciting—she was being stimulated in both holes at the same time.

She moaned. "Ohhhh."

"See? Practicing in ways that feel good is not so ineffective, is it?"

Delia said nothing. She just focused on the pleasure, like Meela had told her. She definitely still felt the plug inside her ass. It felt so good; she thought she was going to come already. But it was like Meela had a sixth sense for these kinds of things. She stopped just before Delia went over the edge of pleasure. Meela kept the dildo stuffed inside Delia, but she did not thrust it. Instead, she leaned back and played with the plug in Delia's ass, pulling it halfway out and pushing it back in. It was driving Delia crazy.

She found herself trying to thrust her cunt backwards against the cock to get herself off, but Meela removed the plug—leaving her ass suddenly empty—and pulled the dildo out of her cunt.

"Are we done practicing already?"

"I think you've had enough."

"No, please, I want to practice more." The truth was Delia wasn't thinking about practicing at all. She just wanted to get her orgasm.

"You want more?"

"Yes, please."

"Okay." Meela spread Delia's ass cheeks apart and pressed the cock against her ass hole. Delia didn't know if she was ready, but Meela applied pressure, and the head of the toy slid inside her. Just like that, it was already in as far as Master Caspius had gotten his cock, albeit this one was considerably less girthy. Meela didn't press the dildo all the way to its full depth. She only inserted it about as far as the butt plug had gone, and then she began making tiny thrusts, not letting the dildo pull all the way out on the back thrusts. Delia was thankful for that because entry was the part that caused the most intense sensation, and she still wasn't entirely used to that feeling.

But what Meela was doing right now felt good. Delia's body was still craving her orgasm. She knew she wouldn't get one from the dildo in her ass, but just feeling something penetrating her was keeping her insanely aroused. Meela kept fucking her ass with those light, tiny thrusts. It felt entirely different from being fucked in the cunt. The newness of the sensation was exciting, and now that the dildo was actually in her, it really did feel good.

On the next thrust, Meela slowly pressed her hips forward, pushing the dildo further inside Delia's ass. Delia gasped at the sensation of the cock sliding into her. It felt...wrong somehow, but in a good way. Like she was doing something to her body that it wasn't intended for but that her body was somehow perfectly made for at the same time. Then Meela began thrusting again, still short, gentle bursts of movement, and Delia felt her clit throbbing for attention.

Meela pulled the dildo most of the way out without removing it and rubbed more lubricant onto its shaft. Then she sank the cock back into Delia's ass, right up to the point she had been before. After a couple of thrusts, Meela pressed the cock all the way into Delia's hole, sinking it in up to the harness. It wasn't a long dildo—only about four inches—but Delia sighed as she felt her body accept all of it. At that point, Meela started fucking her faster, slapping her hips and thighs against Delia's ass cheeks. The intense sensations inside her ass hole increased. The dildo moved in and out of her at its full length, plunging into her ass. And then something happened that Delia had not expected. She felt her whole lower region—her vulva, her vagina, and her ass hole—clench together as her clit throbbed and she came. She came from her ass. And she moaned in pleasure about it. When she quieted, Meela stopped thrusting.

Delia sighed and put her head down on the pillow in front of her. "What the fuck was that?"

"That was you having an anal orgasm."

"I didn't know I could do that."

"Pretty great, huh?"

Delia turned her head and saw Meela grinning smugly.

"You don't have to act so cocky about it just because you fucked me and made me come."

"Oh, okay. I'm cocky, am I? Let's see how cocky I can be." Meela grabbed Delia's hips again and started pounding her in the ass with the tiny dildo. Delia immediately started groaning into her pillow.

"Oh my goodness; it feels so good." Delia could feel herself drooling onto the pillow.

Meela laughed. "Yeah, that's what I thought." Her friend continued banging her in the ass until Delia had come three more times.

After they were done, Meela left the dorm room to go into town with a few other initiates. They were going to the tea shop, which Delia loved, but she decided to stay in. She had practice to do. And a goal to meet. The look on Meela's face said she knew exactly what Delia planned to get up to.

Alone in the dorm room, Delia pulled open the rough, wooden drawer at the top of her dresser and took out her dildos. She had three of them. One of them, she didn't use much anymore. It was about the size of the dildo Meela had used on her ass. There was another that was slightly thicker than that one, but much longer. And then there was her favorite. The Thick Boy. Well, that's what she called it anyway. Thick Boy wasn't as long as her longest dildo, but it didn't need to be. She loved its girth.

Unfortunately, Thick Boy was not the right tool for the job at hand. She set it aside, keeping it in view for motivation towards her goal. It was, after all, about as thick as Master Caspius's girthy cock. Then she set to work with the smallest dildo. After how long Meela had fucked her ass, her hole opened fairly easily for the small dildo. It did, however, amaze her how quickly the muscle would shrink back to its normal size. When she stretched her neck to look down at her hole, it looked just as tight and closed off as ever. She had no idea how Meela—or anyone else for that matter—put such thick objects into their asses.

Instead of lying on her back this time, she squatted on the floor, much like she had seen Meela do that first night with the biggest butt plug. She reached around behind herself and pressed the tip of the dildo between her butt cheeks. She felt excited. Like she had a secret. Like she had felt the first time she'd discovered masturbation. She pushed the dildo into the outside of her tight ass hole, and she tensed up a bit. Entry always felt so intense, almost painful. She took a couple breaths and reminded herself that it was just because she was still tight. The pain didn't mean she was harming herself in any way. Her ass hole would be fine when she was done, and it would go right back to its normal size.

She focused on completely relaxing all of her muscles, including the muscle at the rim of her ass, and pressed the dildo in. She felt her ass immediately clench around the tip. She exhaled. Hoo, it was in. She started working the fake cock further into her ass, a little at a time. She slathered it with more lubricant. Once she'd managed to get it all the way in, she started pumping the dildo into her ass. She'd never known that her ass hole was such a sensitive sexual organ.

She looked down between her legs as she pumped the toy into herself. Interestingly, when she stuffed herself in the ass, her cunt hole gaped open, like it was begging to be filled, itself. Not today.

She couldn't help herself. She started thrusting the dildo into her ass faster, until her hand was thumping against the hardwood floor. She leaned forward, getting onto her knees and leaning on one hand to get the floor or of the way, and she pumped the dildo into her ass wildly.

Suddenly, she felt a huge orgasm building up deep inside her. She leaned further forward onto her hand and pumped the small dildo as deep as it would go into her ass. The hand holding the dildo was tired, but she was so close. She plunged the dildo in and out of her ass, feeling the full length of it tugging at her tight little opening. Her body exploded into orgasm, and she heard the sound of liquid spattering against the floor like someone was pissing on it. In fact, it almost felt like she was pissing and coming at the same time, the way the orgasm burst forth from her. She felt the hot, wet spatters spray against the tops of her thighs and get on the knees of her socks.

Delia held herself there, one hand still clutching the dildo to her ass, laughing. She had squirted. Seriously? All this time trying to unlock that secret, and it turned out that all she needed was a cock up her ass. Yup. She was addicted. She couldn't help herself. Once she realized she could squirt from fucking herself in the ass, she put more lubricant on the dildo and pumped it into herself until the hot fluids squirted out of her again, soaking the floor and her socks.

She dropped onto the floor, letting her belly splatter in the mess she had made. She lay there, panting from the exertion. She put her hand down to feel the mixture of thick cum and watery squirt both seeping from her cunt, and she rubbed the two fluids together, relishing just how wet she was. She laughed in exultation. There was no way she wasn't getting the demo position. She stood up to get a towel and the medium-sized plug. She figured she was ready for it now that her ass was loosened up.

CHAPTER EIGHT

A Selfless Instructor

By the time Meela got back to the room, Delia had trained herself to the girth of the medium plug—one and three-quarter inches. She was easily able to put it in and out, and when the door opened and Meela came in, Delia was lying on her bed, exhausted, clenching her ass hole around the hefty plug to feel it taking up space in her ass.

Meela looked at her. "Wow. You look tired."

Delia just nodded and didn't respond.

"I brought you back some tea you can make in the room." Meela crept over to Delia's dresser and placed a small package on top.

"Thanks."

"You, uh...you okay?"

She smiled. "I'm great! I can fit in the medium plug."

"I see that. You really are determined, aren't you?"

She got up on her elbows to look at her friend. "Yes. I am going to get that demo position. And I am going to train my ass faster than any initiate ever has. Wanna help some more?"

"No, I'm tired, but I thought you might ask, so I brought someone else to help out." Meela went back over to the door. "You can come in."

Delia scrambled to sit up so that whoever it was didn't just walk in to the sight of her legs spread open on the bed. She swiped at the sweaty strands of hair around her face and sticking to her cheeks, trying to make herself look less like she had spent the day fucking herself silly. At least she'd taken the time to clean up all the squirt from the floor.

"Hello, Delia."

She looked up at the figure standing in the door. "Instructor Pratom?" She didn't know what to say. Her instructor in Selflessness stood just inside the doorway of her dorm room. He pushed up the glasses on his nose.

"Yes, well, Meela is one of my best students, and when she told me how hard you were working toward your goal, I couldn't help but want to assist in any way I could."

Delia nodded. Sex between students and instructors was fairly common at DS Academy, but typically it was one of the Dominant instructors who paired with submissive initiates. "Is your..." She felt strange asking the question. "Is your Dominant okay with you doing this?"

Instructor Pratom grinned. "Oh goodness yes. I don't do anything without Mistress Canabella's permission. We have an arrangement regarding my role with students."

She nodded again. "Well, okay then. Thanks for coming to help."

Instructor Pratom continued standing at the door. He was somewhere between average and tall height with warm, medium-dark skin and a wide jaw that made him look like a chipmunk with its cheeks stuffed full. His dark, kinky hair was cut close to his head. And he was still just standing there. At first, it made Delia feel awkward, but now she was getting impatient. She only had so much time to train, and she wasn't going to sit here letting awkwardness eat up her time.

"Well, get over here, then!" She didn't mean to snap at the instructor, but it just came out that way.

Instructor Pratom jumped into action, trotting across the room to her. Meela closed the door behind him and then went about her own business on the other side of the room, ignoring them.

Delia rolled over onto her hands and knees, and using her newly trained anal muscles, squeezed the medium plug out of her ass. It popped out of her hole and clattered to the floor. "Lube's on the nightstand." She gestured toward the small, wooden box that served as a nightstand next to her mattress.

"Oh. Oh my. Just like that then?"

"Yes, go ahead and fuck me. In the ass," she added, in case it wasn't clear.

Instructor Pratom seemed to enjoy being ordered around. He was ready to perform immediately, almost like he'd been trained to do so on command. It was pretty impressive, but Delia didn't tell him so. On her hands and knees, she looked over her shoulder to watch the instructor slather his cock in lubricating balm. It turned her on. Plus, she was relieved to see that Instructor Pratom's dick was average-sized, only a bit girthier than the dildo Meela had used on her, and about an inch longer. She wondered if Meela had known ahead of time that Instructor Pratom's cock would be a size she could take. Then she wondered how Meela would have known that. And then she wondered just how close of friends Instructor Pratom and his "best students" actually were.

Before she could wonder anything further, Instructor Pratom leaned in and pressed his tongue against her ass hole, circling it around the rim. She shivered at the sensation. Then he stuck the tip of his tongue inside her freshly-stretched hole. It sunk right in, and the instructor began plunging his tongue in and out of her ass, pressing his face against her butt cheeks. He made delighted sounds as he did so, as though he were devouring a rich, sweet dessert.

"Mmm. Mmm. Mmm." Instructor Pratom lapped at the inner rim of her butt hole, grabbing her by the thighs and pulling her ass closer into his face. His glasses were probably all smudged up, but he didn't seem to care. The instructor pulled his face away from her ass and leaned in against her on his knees, letting his erect cock slide up under her vulva. He pressed his hips up against her in small movements, teasing at her clit with the shaft of his cock. The Instructor of Selflessness pulled back a bit and let his cock slide up along her wet labia until he positioned it between her ass cheeks.

Delia moaned, waiting for the sensation of being filled. She heard the sound of something clattering onto the nightstand. Instructor Pratom's glasses. He could probably see better without them on at this point, after his enthusiastic rimming. He held his cock pressed against her entrance, and her now-greedy, open ass hole flexed against it, threatening to pull it in without any effort from the instructor.

Tentatively, Instructor Pratom pressed his cock into her ass. It met only slight resistance before sinking halfway in. Still, the instructor did not plunge the whole length in at once. He started with slow, gentle thrusts. Having a real cock inside her definitely felt different from thrusting into herself with a dildo. Delia felt her clit getting engorged at the sensation. Her pussy was dripping.

Instructor Pratom worked his way into her ass a little at a time, steadily sinking in deeper and deeper until he had pressed the full length of his cock inside her. Delia moaned. It felt like he was so deep inside her ass. She bowed down on the mattress, pressing her chest down and keeping her ass thrust up into the air. The instructor grabbed her by the hips and began pumping into her ass harder. Steady, rhythmic thumps. Each time, he pulled back so far that his cock almost came out of her ass, but not quite. And that meant that with each inward thrust, she took the full length of his cock back into her all at once. She could feel the wet secretions of her cunt all over Instructor Pratom's pubic hair as it plapped against her ass.

The instructor didn't fuck her fast. He just kept up that deep, steady rhythm. It made the orgasm inside her build up slowly and intensely, and when she finally came, it rocked through her whole body, wave after wave of orgasms, her thick, creamy cum smearing all over Instructor Pratom's balls as they slapped against her cunt.

When the Instructor of Selflessness stopped, Delia found herself panting against her pillow, completely out of breath. She closed her eyes. "Did you finish?"

"Oh, goodness no. I'm under strict chastity orders. Mistress Canabella allows me to assist my students with their own orgasms, but I am not allowed to cum in them, or with them at all. Or by myself, for that matter." Instructor Pratom chuckled. Then, he slowly pulled his still-erect penis out of Delia's ass. She gasped a little and opened her eyes when the tip finally popped out of her.

"That must be tough."

"Oh, my Lady makes it worthwhile." Instructor Pratom grinned at her with his full, chipmunk cheeks.

Delia nodded absently. She wondered what control her future Dominant would have over her. It was incredible, really, the things a Dominant could make a submissive do. Willingly. Happily, even, if Instructors Pratom and Lau'Ronya were to be believed.

She'd gotten a little taste of that power herself when Instructor Pratom eagerly hopped to her commands. It must take great restraint to be a good Dominant—to stop oneself from ordering a submissive to go a step too far. She thought about the difference between Master Caspius and Initiate Gordaun, and she felt a small amount of understanding in the Dominant initiate's behavior. He'd been given a taste of power, but he did not truly wield it. He was insecure with it. He was on the lowest rung of the Dominant ladder. It must frustrate him in a way that most submissive initiates don't have to deal with. Delia could certainly understand, however, the climb to be the best.

She thanked Instructor Pratom and let him out the door. Much as she would like to practice all night, she needed to get some rest. But, after he left, as she was about to snuff out the lone candle on her nightstand, the startling sound of a fist pounding on the dorm room door made her jump and drop the candle snuffer. It clacked to the floor. The door shook as the fist pounded several times again.

She looked over at Meela, as though her roommate might know why someone was banging down their door in the night. Meela's gray-green eyes were wide, her shoulders raised, and her body shrunken in on itself. The other woman stared back at her, unmoving, so Delia crept toward the door. As she got close, the banging came again, three loud pounds, their thin door jumping with each bang.

Now that she was closer to the door, she could hear the Head Submissive pleading with someone. "This really isn't the time or the place."

The voice that came next was loud, aggressive. Delia recognized it right away. "I will speak with the initiate tonight."

She whispered to herself, "Master Caspius," and pulled the door open. In the hallway, Head Submissive Bandu stood to the side and behind the Dominant instructor. Several nearby doors were open, presumably with various submissive initiates peeking out the cracks to see what was going on. And directly in front of her, Master Caspius stood, hands on his hips, a scowl on his reddened face. He was pissed.

CHAPTER NINE

Selection Process

Delia didn't know what she'd been expecting when she first heard Master Caspius's voice on the other side of the door. What she'd hoped was that he had reconsidered, that he was drawn to her, too, and that he'd come to offer her the demo position. Of course, she knew that was a ridiculous daydream. That couldn't be the real reason he was at her door at night.

And now that she faced him, seeing his nostrils flare and his lips pressed together as he stared down at her, she bit her lower lip and cowered a bit. Was this about her eagerness during Obedience class? Or her questions? She hadn't interacted with the Master of Anal Technique since their depressing meeting in the Head Master's office.

Master Caspius charged a single step forward into her doorway, getting down into her face. "You."

Delia cowered further back, not wanting to step away from him because it would be disrespectful. Instead, she was leaning as far back as she could without falling backwards. She could feel his hot breath rushing down onto her forehead and into her eyes. She blinked several times.

Behind the Dominant instructor, the Head Submissive raised his voice—at least, as much as Head Submissive Bandu could raise his voice. "Master Caspius, please." The Head Submissive was a generally placid man. He didn't yell at the taller man in front of him; he merely projected his voice a bit louder, yet still calm. Delia caught a glimpse of Head Submissive Bandu peeking around from behind Master Caspius. The leader of the College of Submission was a man of average height. He shaved his head and wore the raiment of a monk. He was not weak, however, under his robes. The Head Submissive cultivated his body for the use of his Dominant.

Head Submissive Bandu inserted his body perpendicular to the Dominant instructor's in the doorway. "I think we can discuss this within the initiate's dorm."

Bandu edged his way in around Master Caspius, who was taking up most of the doorway with his hands on his hips and his elbows jutting out to the sides. Head Submissive Bandu came up next to her and put an arm around her shoulders. Delia felt herself relax a little. She didn't know what this was about, but she was grateful that the Head Submissive was here. Master Caspius charged past them into the room, and Delia reached out, hand trembling, to close her door. She could see the other initiates watching the encounter from the hallway, and that made her body tense up even more, her face getting hot from the implied wrong she had done, that everyone now knew about. She bit her lower lip again, pressing down hard. She relaxed her jaw, leaving an indent on the lip, and then she inhaled deeply and lifted her chin high as she closed the door.

As soon as she had closed the door and turned around, Master Caspius charged toward her from across the room. "You have been interfering with my class demonstration." He stuck a long, slender finger into her face.

Delia opened her mouth to respond, but she was at a loss for words. Her mouth simply gaped.

Head Submissive Bandu interjected calmly. "Delia, is this true?"

She tore her eyes away from the blazing twin storms of Master Caspius's and looked into Bandu's soothing lakes of blue-green. They were almost like Meela's eyes, but not quite the same up close.

"All I did was audition for the anal demo position." She cast her eyes downward. "And I failed miserably at it." She raised her eyes up again to meet Bandu's, biting her lip to keep from crying. "I haven't done anything since then, except practice my anal training, but that hasn't interfered with Master Caspius in any way. I haven't been anywhere near him, except when he came to talk in the Obedience class I'm taking." She looked over at Master Caspius, scowling, furious at the vulnerable position he'd put her in. "I have no idea what he's talking about right now."

Master Caspius straightened his posture to his full height and put his hands back on his hips. "Because of you, I cannot get the demo submissive that I need for my class demonstration." He removed his left hand from its hip and, without looking, gestured behind him toward Meela's bed. Delia turned her attention to her roommate. Meela was sitting on her bed, knees and blanket pulled up to her chest, a terrified look on her face. But through the terror, as Meela made eye contact with her, Delia could see almost a pleading look in her friend's eyes, a look of guilt.

Delia was confused. She cocked her head to the side. "I don't understand. Meela?"

Meela burst into tears. "I'm so sorry, Delia! I was just trying to help. I didn't mean to mess things up for you." Meela began sobbing, pulling the blanket up into her face.

Master Caspius addressed Head Submissive Bandu. "That initiate over there came to me to audition for the demo position I have available, and she did an outstanding job. I offered her the position on the spot, and she refused me. I asked her why she would audition for a position that she didn't intend to fill, and she said she never expected that she would actually get the position; she had auditioned to find out what her friend needed to be able to do to succeed." Master Caspius shoved a finger in the air in front of Delia's face once again. "This friend."

Bandu put a finger and thumb to his chin. "Hmm. I can see why you are frustrated, Master Caspius. Of course, if the initiate—"Head Submissive Bandu swept his arm in Meela's direction—"does not wish to participate in the demonstration, that is her choice."

Master Caspius took an audible breath. "Yes, of course it is her choice, Head Submissive. My complaint is that her choice is being swayed by this interloper."

Meela stood up on her mattress, blankets still clutched in her fingers but dropped down away from her face, which was puffy and streaked with wetness. "Oh, no, Head Submissive, that is not true. I have no intention of performing as a demo submissive, even if Delia didn't want the position herself."

Master Caspius threw his hands up in the air. "But why not? You are the best anal bottom I have seen perform in quite a while. You're perfect for the position."

Meela dropped her head, looking down at her mattress. Master Caspius made an exasperated sound.

Delia looked from the Instructor of Anal Technique to her friend. She felt her dream being pulled away from her. She took a full breath. "Meela, if you are really that qualified for the position, you should take it. You deserve it. Not me."

Master Caspius raised an eyebrow as he looked down at her. "Suddenly you don't want the position?"

Delia looked him full in the eyes, all the fire of her desire behind her eyes. "No, Sir. I do want the position. And I know that I could succeed at it."

Meela leapt over to them, looking up at Master Caspius and appealing to him. "It's true, Sir! She's done nothing but practice anal training in her spare time since she came home from that audition with you. I've been helping her."

Master Caspius raised his eyebrows appraisingly. "I'm sure your instruction has helped her."

Meela nodded her head vigorously. "She's making faster progress than I made when I first started training. She'll be better than me in no time."

Master Caspius nodded his head at Meela. Then he turned to Delia and looked down his narrow nose at her. He smiled, the storms in his eyes turning to sprinkles. "You will never be the demo submissive for my class." His grin broadened, and he tapped the black cane—ever at his hand—to the floor. "All right then. My business here is done. Thank you for your time and assistance, Head Submissive Bandu." Master Caspius walked to their dorm room door, whistling, and let himself out.

Delia stared after him, feeling hollow inside. Her mouth hung open. Her eyes felt tired. Her shoulders felt heavy. Gone was all the tension she had been holding in them. Her arms felt like puppet arms from which the strings had been cut. They hung limply, helplessly, at her side. "That's it then?" she mumbled.

Meela came up to her side and touched her arm. "I'm so sorry, Delia."

The kind touch of her friend made something inside her snap. "No." She snatched her arm away from Meela. She softened her voice and repeated herself. "No. There is nothing for you to apologize for, friend. This means nothing. There are words, and there are actions. And when I reach my full potential with anal training, Master Caspius will have no choice but to select me for his demonstration. He doesn't believe in me yet. But he will." Delia smiled at her friend. "With your help, he will. I am continuing with my plan."

Head Submissive Bandu regarded her with a curious look on his face. But he only said, "Get your rest, initiates." He bowed to them, inclining his head. "I'd like to get back to my regular duties, if you are done with my assistance."

"Yes, of course, Head Submissive." Delia let him out the door. After, she turned back into her room, energy pulsing through her small body. She felt pumped up, larger than usual. She had been offered a challenge, and she was convinced that that was exactly what Master Caspius had intended. He wanted to piss her off so that she would try even harder.

Meela looked at her, much like a squirrel might eye a nearby hound. "Are...are you okay?"

Delia grinned, all her teeth showing. "Yes. Yes, I am. Get my box of butt plugs for me. We have more practice to do tonight." Meela practically leapt across the room with her long legs. And Delia continued grinning to herself, knowing she would put Master Caspius in his place. She was the best, and she would show him.

CHAPTER TEN

The Big Plug

The next day, Delia skipped classes. She had stayed up most of the night with Meela, who had helped her to get the second to largest butt plug into her ass. It really was a lot easier to take a plug when someone else was pushing it in. The idea of the other person enjoying filling her ass turned her on. She liked to think about a cock pressing its way into her hole, thrusting in whether she was ready or not, the other person simply taking what they wanted from her. Keeping that fantasy in her head made her ass open up for the large, two-inch plug. She was getting eager to make another attempt at the audition with Master Caspius, but she wasn't ready quite yet. She wanted to be able to take the largest plug before she made her second attempt.

Realistically, Delia knew that the second-largest plug was probably about the same girth as the Instructor of Anal Technique's cock, but training to a bit larger size would make the audition easier and would allow her to show Master Caspius that she could take his cock with ease. She wouldn't have to struggle at all. As she lay in bed, she smiled to herself, thinking about what his reaction would be, and how he would have no choice but to accept her as his demo submissive. Not only would Meela—the best anal bottom in the College of Submission—not accept the role, but Delia would outperform Meela. She would, herself, become the best in the university.

Despite the two of them only getting a couple hours of sleep by the time they were done practicing, Meela had gotten up and gone to her first class anyway. It was funny. Even though Meela had taunted her about being a good girl that first night they practiced together, Meela was, in fact, the ultimate good girl submissive. Or at least she would be if she could only get over performing in front of people.

Delia stretched out in bed, enjoying the feeling of breaking a rule and skipping class. She learned a lot in her classes, but nothing was more important right now than achieving the goal in front of her, and she was going to get there today. This is what it meant to be the best — to cast aside all the unnecessary obstacles in the way and focus on accomplishing what needed to be done. After the couple hours of sleep, she was still tired, but sunlight was pouring into the room through the window — that bright sunlight that bounces off snow, somehow seeming brighter than even the summer's sun. She wouldn't be able to sleep with the sun shining into her eyes, and she was glad for it.

The box of butt plugs still lay next to her on the floor, where Meela had left them after loosening Delia's ass with them all night. She reached over into the box and pulled out the largest plug, holding it in her hand. She thought back to the night she had held the smallest plug, feeling its weight. Like that one, this butt plug was made of solid steel. It was fairly hefty. Delia watched the sunlight glint off it, like a trophy she was about to win. The largest plug was a girthy two and quarter inches in diameter, but — well-stretched from the night before — she was confident that she could take it.

Delia rolled over onto her side. It was her new favorite position for solo anal play. With her legs together and her knees bent so that her ass was thrust out towards the edge of the bed, she slathered the large plug in lubricating balm. Once she had it completely covered to her satisfaction, she reached around her side and smeared the extra lube onto the outside of her ass hole.

She directed the tapered end of the plug toward her not-so-tight opening. The familiar press of a heavy object against her ass hole sent a thrill through her. She was immediately turned on. Her ass accepted the narrow end of the big plug greedily, and she pushed it in until she reached the point of resistance, just before the widest part of the plug. The first time getting the widest point of a new plug inside her was always a little difficult, but now she knew the right techniques for easing it in. Meela had been right. Anal training wasn't meant to be a struggle. Struggling only made the muscle tighten up.

Instead, as she reached the point of resistance, Delia focused on how good the part of the plug that was already inside her felt. She let her mind greedily wander to how good it would feel when the rest of that thick plug was inside her ass. She imagined a greedy lover desperately wanting inside of her, pressing a girthy cock firmly into her, as she rhythmically thrust the plug against her resisting ass. She worked it up inside her, not worrying about whether she would get it in, instead, only enjoying the feeling of its entrance. She slid the plug most of the way back out and then plunged it back in to the point of resistance again, working the lube around inside her.

She did this several more times and then applied a steady pressure to the plug with the heel of her hand, breathing and focusing on relaxing the muscle near the rim of her ass. With a grunt and a moan, the large plug sunk into her. "Ohhhhh." She squeezed her ass around it, taking in the delicious feeling of having her ass so full of thick metal.

Delia just lay there for a moment, relishing her accomplishment. She had done it. She'd successfully trained her ass to take the largest butt plug in her set. She took in a little sighing breath, feeling the weight of all that steel in her ass. The accomplishment was sweet, but it was no longer enough for her. She grabbed the steel plug by the protruding handle and began pumping it into her ass—not pulling it out, just shoving it up inside her with little thrusts—feeling her cunt leak with each pump. Gradually, she worked her way up to pulling the thick, maximum diameter of the plug up and out of her ass hole and pushing it back in, feeling the thickest part of the plug stretch her hole open. The more she pulled it out and pushed it back in, the looser her hole was getting, the more accommodating it became.

She stopped thrusting the handle with her hand but kept her palm against the end of it and started using her internal muscles to squeeze the thick plug out of her ass. Then, she would plunge it back in with her palm. She kept doing that, pushing the plug out, catching it in her palm, and shoving it back inside her.

When her hole was good and loosened, she pulled the butt plug all the way out of her ass and started plunging it into her all at once and pulling it all the way back out again. She moaned and wriggled around on the bed. Her hole was so loose that she could repeatedly plunge the entire large plug into her gaping ass and pull it back out. She fucked herself in the ass with the girthy, steel plug until she felt the hot stream of her squirt pumping out of her, and even then, she kept on plunging the hot steel into her ass. Every time she thrust the thick toy into herself, another stream of squirt ejected from her body, soaking the bed. She didn't care. It felt too good to care. She plunged the toy into her ass until she'd ejaculated every drop of squirt inside her, until she had nothing left to squirt out of her, and she lay there, soaked, exhausted, her ass a gaping, open hole. She flopped over onto her belly and reached behind her, probing several fingers into her ass, and she laughed in delight at the lack of resistance they received.

She was ready. She looked out the window. She'd been so busy she hadn't been paying attention to the bells or how many times they had sounded. Judging by the sun, it was about lunchtime. Master Caspius would still be teaching classes. She got up and teetered over to the pitcher and basin of water they kept for washing their hands and faces and wiped herself down with a wet cloth. Her legs trembled beneath her, weak from all the coming she had done. Then she dressed quickly, and she headed out to the common area downstairs to get some lunch. She would need her energy for her second shot at the demo submissive audition.

After eating, Delia felt stronger, and her legs had stopped trembling. She had decided to go to her afternoon classes. There was no point in skipping them. After all, she'd accomplished her goal—or at least she would accomplish the last step to it easily now that she'd completed her training. She walked to Obedience class with her head high, pride radiating from her being. She felt like everyone who looked at her could feel it.

In class, they were still covering the topic of respect, but Delia had grown bored with it. While Instructor Lau'Ronya bounced around the front of class like a bubble dancing in the wind, Delia flipped through the Obedience textbook, looking ahead to see what the other tenets of obedience were. According to the book that Instructor Lau'Ronya had literally written, the next steps were to learn to relinquish control of others, become a good receiver, be vulnerable with your Dominant, and practice gratitude. They had just talked about gratitude the other day. Some of these directives seemed kind of repetitive. Delia felt her mind wandering, wondering what the point of it was. She wanted to be a good submissive, of course. But she didn't want to look like some kind of mindless puppet, like the instructor, always laughing at things the Dominants say and telling them how smart they are and never arguing with them even when they say something utterly stupid.

Letting someone be an idiot without correcting them, that's what was really stupid. By the time class was over, Delia was not feeling the idea of going to Selflessness class. She marched down the hall and out into the cold air of the campus quad and took in a breath of freedom. She wanted to see what the Dominant initiates were learning. So she headed off down the trail that led to the College of Dominance, determined to sneak a peek at their training.

CHAPTER ELEVEN

A Woman's Touch

Delia stood once again before the large, looming main building at the College of Dominance. In the daylight, it still looked just as imposing, though perhaps a bit less eerie. The dark, gray bricks looked stolid in the sunlight, immoveable. The red bricks around the windows and doors, however, seemed to add a bit of brightness to the aesthetic, like a rush of blood rising to one's cheeks when excited. She marched toward the entrance, knowing she would stand out in her submissive's uniform. She didn't care. She had just as much right to walk through the halls as anyone else did, and not a single initiate in this building had the right to order her around. She didn't belong to them. Right now, as an uncollared initiate, she belonged only to herself.

Fuck the Dominant initiates, she thought. They think they're better than me. They can't touch me.

The large, main doors loomed over her head. She flung one of the doors open and stepped inside, stomping the snow off her boots on the entry rug. The halls were empty again, just like the first night she'd come here. All of the initiates would be in their classes right now. She grinned, knowing she had the halls of the College of Dominance to herself. She felt like a mouse that had eaten its way into the walls.

She stepped down the hallway, not creeping, but not being overly loud. When she came to the first door on her left, she pressed herself up against the wall and listened in. She didn't recognize the voice of the instructor inside this room. It sounded like a woman, and she was instructing the initiates on the proper use of a whip. Not when to use it, but how. The door was fully closed, as was to be expected, so Delia couldn't see anything that was happening within, but she could hear the whip snap against an object—the floor? A chair? The sound excited her.

She made her way along the hall, listening at various doors. Inside one room, an instructor was talking about dignity, in another, about being nurturing. Delia was surprised by that one. She hadn't thought of Dominants as being nurturing before. The next door she came to was not closed all the way. She sidled up to it and listened in. Her breath caught in her throat as she listened. The instructor seemed to be giving instruction on anal techniques, but it wasn't Master Caspius. The voice belonged to yet another woman instructor in the College of Dominance. Delia was intrigued. She crouched down and pried the door open a bit further, holding her breath and hoping that it wouldn't make a noise. She only opened it a crack, just enough to peek into the room, but the door, like all of those in this building, was heavy, and it creaked as she cracked it open. Her shoulders tensed up, and she waited. A couple of students' heads turned toward the door— those near the back of the class—but they couldn't see her through the small opening, and they shortly turned their attention back to the instructor at the front of the room.

Delia let out the breath she'd been holding and put her eye up close to the crack between the door and its frame. At the front of the class, the instructor was dressed in a red corset top and black leather pants. Over the pants, she wore a red harness, and as she paced the front of the room, lecturing to the students, a strap-on dildo wagged around in front of her. As Delia listened, the instructor used the word "pegging" several times. She was familiar with the term. It was what Meela had done with her. But Delia didn't know there were entire classes on it.

She watched, mesmerized, as the pegging instructor called students up to the front of the class. Each student wielded a strapon. On the instructor's desk was what appeared to be some kind of large, stuffed doll made to look like a naked man, laying ass-up over the desktop. It was like the biggest rag doll she'd ever seen. It wasn't particularly lifelike. Each student would practice going up to the doll and inserting their strapon in a hole in the doll that Delia couldn't see. She must have watched this for about fifteen minutes, student after student penetrating the lifeless doll, when she realized that classes would probably be letting out soon. She didn't want to still be in the hallway when all the Dominant initiates started pouring out into it. She stood up, stretching the tightness out of her muscles from crouching so long, and let the door fall back to mostly closed.

Just as the small crack in the door vanished, it reappeared, and someone from inside the classroom pulled the door all the way open. Delia froze. As she stood in the doorway, the entire class full of Dominant initiates had their heads turned toward her, as did the instructor at the front of the room.

The Instructor of Pegging beamed at her. "Submissive. Welcome. Enter the room, please."

Delia stepped inside, the confidence she'd felt upon entering the hallway fleeing from her. Beside her, an initiate who had opened the door now closed it.

The Instructor of Pegging spoke again. "Of course I've been aware of you listening at our door. A curious little thing you are. Adorable. I like a submissive with a bit of devious curiosity." The instructor beckoned her forward, and Delia started walking to the front of the room, glancing to her sides and noting that the majority of the students in this class were female.

"Tell me, little initiate, do you like anal play?"

Delia looked at the Dominant instructor and nodded with a few small, quick movements of her head. She licked her lips, which had suddenly gone dry, and wondered if she'd be in trouble for listening in.

The instructor, however, sounded pleased when she spoke. "Wonderful! Maybe you would like to help out some of my students with their practice. It can be so hard to find enough bottoms to practice with, and they often end up practicing on these ridiculous dolls." The instructor gestured to the rag doll on the desk. "Not exactly inspiring, is it?"

Delia had reached the front of the class and stood before the instructor, a woman several inches taller than herself. She looked over at the doll and shook her head. The instructor gazed at her, her brown eyes shimmering. "Will you help us?" The Instructor of Pegging held out a red, leather-gloved hand toward her.

Delia swallowed. Her whole throat was dry. She reached her hand out toward the outstretched hand of the instructor and stepped forward. Her fingertips felt the supple leather grip them and give a reassuring squeeze. The instructor's dark, calming eyes were hypnotic. Then, the instructor let her hand go and in one swoop flung the rag doll off the top of the desk. "Your place, sweet lady."

Delia felt her breath rush into her lungs in several short, excited inhales. She didn't dare look out at the classroom to see how many people were watching. This is what she had trained for. There was no way Master Caspius would be able to turn her down after she'd actually performed as an anal demo submissive. She could even get this instructor to say a good word for her to Master Caspius. She couldn't believe her luck.

She leaned forward over the edge of the desk and raised her tunic up over her ass, thrusting it out. The Instructor of Pegging chuckled and spoke to her initiates. "Look how eager she is."

Several people laughed, but Delia didn't care. They wouldn't be laughing when they saw what she could do.

"Let's begin. Avelia, you're first."

As Delia lay against the hard, uncomfortable desktop, she felt a smallish dildo poke awkwardly at her hole. It wasn't exactly thrilling. The initiate seemed to be having some trouble positioning her fake cock. Delia tried to reposition herself on the desktop to make it easier for the Dominant initiate, but the young woman must have been nervous. She couldn't seem to control where she was sticking it. As she pushed the lubricated dildo into Delia, it slipped and ended up sinking into her cunt. The initiate didn't seem to notice that she'd hit the wrong spot and, excited at her apparent success, started thrusting into Delia, who didn't know what to say at this development. In private, she would have told the woman she'd missed the mark, but she figured it wasn't a good idea to call out a Dominant's error—even if they were an initiate—in front of an entire room of other Dominant types.

Fortunately, the instructor saw what was going on and called her to a stop. The initiate pulled the dildo out of Delia's cunt, and the instructor told her to try again. Delia didn't like the feel of someone inexperienced probing around at her ass, so as the Dominant initiate pressed into her again, Delia reached around behind herself and grabbed the dildo, pressing it into her ass hole herself. The initiate made an indignant sound, but the instructor just laughed. "What do you expect, Avelia, when you can't deliver? Okay, next."

Without any decorum, the embarrassed initiate yanked the dildo out of Delia's ass. Good thing it was small. Delia was starting to realize that initiates, Dominant or not, were nothing to be scared of. These people weren't particularly confident. Not yet, anyway. It was interesting to see that Dominant initiates sometimes floundered as much as the submissives did about how to fill their role.

The next initiate did a better job. She lined up her dildo and plunged it in all the way to the harness in one thrust.

The instructor interrupted her. "Whoa! I hope everyone saw that because that is a great example of exactly what not to do. Unless you are certain that your submissive is well trained and warmed up, you should never sink a cock in to the hilt."

"She didn't seem to mind," the initiate standing behind Delia said.

"But a less experienced submissive will mind," the instructor replied. "If you don't know a submissive well, you always assume they need a slow entry."

Delia beamed to herself, cheek pressed against the desktop and looking away from the watching initiates. The Instructor of Pegging considered her an experienced anal submissive. That would show Master Caspius.

The Instructor of Pegging then called up the next initiate to practice. This one seemed to have paid attention to the previous two initiates' failures. She lined up her dildo well and entered Delia's ass with a firm, steady press forward, stopping about halfway in to pull it back and allow the lubricant to be spread around inside her. The instructor allowed this initiate to continue, and Delia's ass greedily accepted the thrusts of the small dildo inside her. She turned her face to the other side, looking out at the initiates who had come here to learn to peg and were now watching her get fucked in the ass. Most of them were women.

Delia had performed sexually in groups before. It wasn't

uncommon in the courses assigned to submissives. But this was the most prolonged sexual act she had put on in front of such a large group, especially one where she was the center of attention. All the eyes on her made her moan. Yes, she would love being the demo submissive in Master Caspius's class. She was certain that the feats required of his demo submissive would be more challenging than the small dildos the initiates in this pegging class were equipped with. She closed her eyes and listened to the sound of the young woman's hips slapping into her ass.

Before she was able to enjoy it too much, though, the instructor congratulated the initiate on a job well done and directed her to stop. This initiate had the decency to remove her cock slowly rather than abruptly ripping it from Delia's body. Still, she felt a slight disappointment at no longer being filled, especially since she hadn't had any orgasms. She supposed, however, that being an anal demo submissive probably wasn't about her getting to come. She wondered if there was some kind of rule about that.

Leaving her folded over the edge of the desk, the Instructor of Pegging began explicating the initiates' homework assignment. Delia wondered if there was some kind of protocol for what she was supposed to do now, but the whole thing had been rather impromptu, so she took it upon herself to quietly stand up and put her tunic back in place. Her moment of attention was over, and the Dominant initiates were all gathering their things and preparing to leave. Bells started to chime from somewhere in the large building. Delia didn't want to be out in the halls, standing out in her submissive's tunic, so she hung back, waiting for the class to clear.

After most of the initiates were gone, the instructor turned to her. "Thank you for your assistance today. I'm Mistress Deblis."

"It was my pleasure. I'm happy to serve. Actually, I have a favor to ask of you."

Mistress Deblis raised an eyebrow. "Did you come here specifically to see me?"

"No, I happened upon your class by chance, but it was fortunate for me. You see, I'm auditioning for demo submissive for Master Caspius's class, and—"

The Dominant instructor interrupted her. "Wait a minute. Is your name Delia D'Morn?"

She nodded her head slowly. "Yes...how did you guess that?"

Mistress Deblis threw her head back and laughed. "Are you wanting me to put in a good word for you with Master Caspius?"

Delia didn't understand what was funny. Warily, she answered. "...Yes."

Mistress Deblis put a red-gloved hand on her shoulder, still chuckling to herself. "You did a great job in my class today, and I'm grateful, but nothing I say will get you into the good graces of Master Caspius. You've become infamous among the instructors here, after Caspius's rants about you interfering in his demo submissive search."

Delia's face grew hot, and she shrunk away from the hand on her shoulder. "What do you mean?"

"I mean that you are welcome to demo in my class any time, but other instructors here may be more wary of your presence at the College of Dominance."

Delia backed away. "Master Caspius will change his mind. I don't need your word with him to get the position."

Mistress Deblis adjusted her gloves and shrugged. "Suit yourself. You're not my submissive. I can't tell you what to do."

Delia started toward the door of the classroom. The sounds outside the room had calmed, but this was the last period for daytime courses, and if the College of Dominance was like the College of Submission, there would be another hour before any evening courses started. Delia's sidetrack into the pegging class meant that she wouldn't have the halls to herself now as she made her way up to the instructors' offices. She sighed and turned back to Mistress Deblis.

"Would you assist me with one thing, then? A return-favor for providing uncollared services to you today?"

The Dominant woman smiled down at her. "What would you like?"

Delia stalled for a moment, annoyed that she needed assistance merely for traveling the halls. "Could you please escort me to Master Caspius's office? You don't have to say anything to him about me."

Mistress Deblis came up to her, stalking like a predatory cat on her svelte, leather-clad legs, and linked arms with Delia. "I'd be delighted to escort a pretty little thing like you."

CHAPTER TWELVE

A New Kind of Submission

"You! Why are you in my office?"

Mistress Deblis giggled behind Delia, watching from outside the door. Master Caspius's turned his glare to the other Dominant. "Did you put her up to this?"

"No, the little submissive wished to see you. I merely gave her safe passage through our halls. And now I'm staying to watch the show."

"There is no show. Take her back out of here."

Delia clenched her fists. "No. I am qualified for the demo position, and I am going to audition."

The storms in Master Caspius's eyes blazed as he turned to look at her. "You already auditioned. You failed. And I told you to stay out of the College of Dominance. Yet here you are, disobeying me."

Delia held her chin up high. "As you, yourself, pointed out the first time I saw you, you have no right to order me. I am not your submissive. That's what you told your initiates, and now you're breaking your own rules."

Mistress Deblis guffawed behind her. "She's got you there, Caspius." Master Caspius flared his eyes at the other Dominant. "Close the door and go take care of your own initiates!"

Mistress Deblis shrugged and reached into the room, pulling the door closed. As Delia watched her go, she saw the Instructor of Pegging give her a wink. Delia blinked and turned back to the very angry Instructor of Anal Technique towering over her, breathing roughly through his nostrils. She stood her ground. Gradually, Master Caspius's breathing calmed. He sat down on the small couch in his office, relaxing into the seat and spreading his knees.

"Fine. You want another audition?"

Delia nodded.

"And if I find you unsuitable, will you leave me alone?"

She hesitated briefly but nodded her head.

Master Caspius shook his head as he began unlacing his leather pants. "Initiates. Always something to prove."

Master Caspius pulled out his cock—his flaccid dick flopping against the leather—and remained seated, reclined on the couch. He put his arms out to the sides, resting them on the couch's back, and leaned his head back, closing his eyes. "Go on and get me ready, then."

Delia paused for a moment, staring, before she realized what he meant. She leapt over to the couch and kneeled between Master Caspius's knees. His cock and balls, having been cooped up in the leather all day, released their scent into the air. Master Caspius's scent was mild and musky, and it drove her wild. She licked the tip of his cock. The skin was warm and soft, and she ran her tongue up and down the length of it. Her mouth filled with saliva at the taste, and as she continued licking his shaft, she spread saliva around it, making his cock slippery. Master Caspius's dick was already starting to wake up, though it wasn't fully erect yet.

At that point, Delia took the Dominant instructor's cock fully in her mouth, pressing her nose down into his pubes. Her mouth was small, but she could take all of his cock while it was only semi-erect. It was, however, already making her open her jaw as wide as she could as it continued to grow in her mouth. She loved that feeling. She pulled her head back away from his cock, making a small, muffled sound and letting a trail of slobber string out of her mouth.

Master Caspius's cock was getting big now, almost to its full length and girth. She wouldn't be able to fit all of it back into her throat—that would be too toothy—so Delia wrapped her lips around half the length, focusing on the end of his shaft with her mouth and stroking the remaining shaft with her hand, which slid smoothly through the trails of saliva she had left behind. She looked up to see Master Caspius's expression. He paid her no attention. His head was still leaned back with his eyes closed. He made no sounds.

She doubled down her efforts, flicking her tongue around his frenulum as she sucked his cock and then removing her hand to thrust his girthy dick as far into the back of her throat as she could, making sure to keep her lips in the way of her teeth as much as possible. As she forced her throat down onto the large cock, she couldn't help emitting a few gagging sounds. Her eyes watered. And when she pulled her head back, sucking just the tip of Master Caspius's cock, she could see bubbles of slobber had been left on the shaft.

At that point, Master Caspius finally spoke. "All right. It's ready for you. Begin your audition."

She looked up at the instructor. He had opened his eyes, but he still sat in the same reclined position. She jumped up from her knees, ready to show him what she could take. Master Caspius did not move from his spot. "Go on, then."

Delia stopped breathing for a bit and looked at him. "What would you like me to do?"

Master Caspius rolled his eyes. "I think it's obvious. I want you to fuck my cock with your ass. You are the one who wants this, so I am going to sit here and relax."

Delia felt her shoulders tense. She'd never done anal like this. She'd only ever had someone fuck her from behind. That's how Master Caspius had done it the first time she auditioned. She wasn't expecting something different this time. It wasn't fair. But she knew she couldn't say that. If an expert at anal sex could do this, then she could do this.

"Umm, should I get the lubricant? Where do you keep it again?"

Master Caspius waved a hand lazily. "No need for lubricant. You've slobbered on it sufficiently."

"But in Anal Training 101 at the College of Submission, they said to always use lubricant."

"And in Advanced Anal Techniques, one learns that well-trained anal bottoms—submissive or otherwise—can take a cock up the ass with saliva as sufficient lubrication." He held her gaze. "Are you well trained, or aren't you?"

Delia scowled at him and stepped forward.

"Ah, ah." Master Caspius made a swirling motion with his finger. "Turn around. I want to be able to watch your technique. Besides, I don't want to have to make eye contact with you."

Delia's mouth dropped open, and she almost retorted, but she stopped herself and bit her lip, feeling the pressure rise in her head. Master Caspius was making her test difficult intentionally. Pissed off, she pulled her tunic up over her head, turned around, and squatted over Master Caspius's lap. She grabbed the Instructor of Anal Technique's cock in her right hand, directing it toward her ass. Balancing herself with one hand on his thigh, she slipped the thick head of his cock between her ass cheeks and sat back forcefully, swallowing his whole cock with her ass in one gulp. She'd been too angry to think about what she was doing. The saliva didn't provide quite as much glide as the lubricating balm did, but it was sufficient to let his cock inside her. She felt her ass being pulled open more intensely than she would have with the lube. There was the sensation of a bit more resistance than she would have liked. Master Caspius's cock was thick and filling, and her hole felt well-stretched around it. Still, she had practiced with plugs large enough to easily accommodate the instructor's size.

She lifted her ass up off his lap and slapped her ass cheeks back down against him, plunging Master Caspius's cock deep into her ass. Now that the saliva was getting good and spread around inside her, she could focus on how amazing it felt to finally have the Dominant instructor's cock in her ass. This is what she'd been waiting for. It was better than any of the training she'd done. Delia closed her eyes and savored the sensation of Master Caspius's cock stretching her open and reaching deep into her belly. She held herself up with one hand on each of his thighs, plapping her ass against his lap.

As she looked down, she could see strings of her own cum hanging from her cunt and sticking to the instructor's leather pants. The sight of her cum turned her on even more, and she raised up her ass, stopping to rub her hand around her vulva and spread her cum onto Master Caspius's cock, providing more lubrication and also giving her the thrill of putting her own cum in her ass. She sat back down, feeling the whole length of his cock get swallowed inside her. Her ass was greedy for it, and she started breathing heavier with the exertion of bouncing up and down on the instructor's dick. She liked this—the feel of a real cock stuffing her ass and control over the tempo. It was like the best of both worlds of being fucked and masturbating.

Delia kept plunging Master Caspius's cock into her, digging her fingers into his thighs. She felt the Dominant instructor tense and flex beneath her, and she felt his cock throbbing in orgasm inside her. Still, he said nothing. She knew he was done, but she could feel his cock hitting that spot deep inside her. She didn't want to stop yet. As Master Caspius's cum began to drip out of her ass and lather his cock with each of her downward thrusts, she was overtaken with all the sensations. She felt her abdomen and the muscles in her ass tense up. Master Caspius groaned as his finished cock continued to be fucked.

He finally spoke. "Okay, you've completed your audition."

She didn't stop. Instead, she said, "Almost." And she spread her legs further apart as she continued to fuck his cock with her ass. She clenched her fingers into his thighs and pressed all of her weight back against him, fucking herself deep in the ass, and then she felt her orgasm burst forth. Delia squirted uncontrollably all over the floor and Master Caspius's low table. Still, she didn't stop. Master Caspius hissed in a breath behind her, but he didn't attempt to remove her from his lap. Delia humped against his cock, each thrust causing another stream of liquid to spurt forth from her body. The squirt spread across the hardwood floor, seeping under the couch and over to Master Caspius's desk. She didn't stop until only little spurts of fluid trickled out and then finally nothing at all.

Then, she leaned back against Master Caspius. It was inappropriate, but she was spent. The instructor breathed heavily behind her, and under her ass, she could feel a puddle of liquid pooled up in the lap of his leather pants. She could also feel Master Caspius's cock starting to shrink inside her. Before the closeness got too awkward, she groaned and stood up, letting his cock slide out of her ass. When the full length of it finally exited her tender, used ass hole, she shivered at the sensation of sudden emptiness.

Carefully, on her trembling legs, she turned around to face the instructor, being careful not to slip in her own squirt. Master Caspius regarded her seriously. "That was impressive. Much more interesting than your first attempt." He shook his head, looking as if he wanted to say something more.

Delia felt exultant. She had done it. She'd made a goal to train her ass to fit Master Caspius, and she had done it. She'd even impressed him. A grin spread across her face. "So I've got the demo position?"

"Absolutely not."

Her grin fell. "What! Why not? You just said my audition was impressive."

"It was, but I'm giving the demo position to someone else. I told you already that I would not be awarding it to you."

"I don't understand."

"It's not really for you to understand. You made this silly test for yourself. It's not my job to indulge you."

Delia clenched her fists. "But I'm better than whoever you gave the position to!"

Master Caspius shrugged and adjusted his shirt, which was not entirely dry at the edges. "Perhaps."

She sputtered. "Then what the hell am I doing here?"

"Proving something to yourself, I presume."

"But it's not worth anything if I don't get the demo position. What can I do to get it?"

Master Caspius sighed and looked up at her from the couch. "Little one, there is nothing you can do. My decision is made." He paused long enough for her to suck in a breath, ready to respond to him. He didn't let her. Instead, he held up a hand and continued to speak. "However. I do have another position that I am in dire need of someone to fill."

Delia stopped the angry response she was holding in and exhaled, cocking her head at the instructor. "Another position?"

"Yes. I'm afraid you won't get the opportunity to perform in front of a class. I can tell you're the kind who likes the attention. But you would be of great use to me. You see, I need a research assistant."

Delia said nothing. She didn't understand what he meant by research assistant. She imagined sitting around in the instructor's office, looking up obscure sexual positions in textbooks. It wasn't exactly the use of her talents she'd been looking for.

"I don't know if that's something I'd be interested in."

Master Caspius furrowed his brow. "Really? I would have thought you'd jump at the chance. Guess I read you wrong. No matter. I'll eventually find someone with the right skill set."

Now Delia furrowed her own brow. "What skill set does the

position require? What would your research assistant need to do?"

Master Caspius looked down and lifted one corner of his mouth in a grin, stroking the gray tip of his beard. "I need someone to practice new techniques with me. The successful applicant would be my personal assistant during my private research hours. After all, as an instructor in Anal Technique, including advanced techniques, I need to keep up on trends in the field. The person who fills the position would be a test subject, of sorts, who would allow me to try out different anal techniques on their person." He looked up at her. "Of course, I need someone willing to try new things and do additional training as necessary. It's quite an exclusive position."

Delia's eyes lit up. "I want it."

Master Caspius chuckled. "Of course you do." He shook his head. "You've caused me a bit of trouble this semester, you know."

Delia got to her knees in the cooling puddle of squirt on the floor. The parts of her socks that hadn't already gotten soggy quickly began absorbing the liquid. "Please, let me make it up to you, Master Caspius. Let me be your test subject. I promise I can take anything that you try on me. You won't find a more willing assistant."

The Dominant instructor regarded her for a moment, making her wait in the wetness. He sighed. "All right, but do not make me regret offering you this boon."

Delia jumped up, splashing wetness around with her socks and grabbing her tunic from the floor beside her. The garment was dripping wet. She bit her lip and looked at Master Caspius. "Sorry about the mess."

"I don't know what you're sorry about. You're going to clean it up before you go."

"Yes, Sir."

"Good girl."

She held up her wet tunic. "Do you have something else I could wear when I leave?"

"No, I do not. You'll just have to wear your cloak with nothing under it when you go." Master Caspius gestured to where her cloak was still hanging beside the door. At least that was still dry. "Now, I do have an evening class to teach shortly, so I'll need you to get this mess cleaned up before I lock up here."

Delia took the towels Master Caspius provided to her and cleaned every surface she had squirted on. When she was done, she walked out of Master Caspius's office, naked under her cloak, socks squelching in her boots, with the satisfying feel of the instructor's cum leaking down her inner thigh.

CHAPTER THIRTEEN

The Teddy Bear

"I am not fucking that thing."

"Well, yes, you are." Master Caspius twirled his black cane around in his fingers. "Otherwise, I will find a better assistant."

Delia gritted her teeth. She felt like she was being humiliated intentionally. Lying on the floor in front of her was a life-sized teddy bear. It was bigger than she was. The bear looked ratty, with nappy fur that appeared to have been touched extensively. It was almost bare in patches. At the stuffed animal's crotch, a secure harness was fastened that would hold various toys Master Casplus wanted to try out. Right now, a fairly average-looking dildo was fastened to its fuzzy crotch.

Delia sighed. "Fine. Whatever you think will make me a better anal submissive. Do I at least get some lube, or do I have to suck off the bear?"

Master Caspius put a gloved finger to his lower lip, frowned, and raised his eyebrows. "You know, I hadn't considered having you suck off the bear, but yes, I'd love to see that."

"Fuck that! I don't have to do everything you tell me. In case you've forgotten your own moral code, I am not your collared submissive."

Master Caspius laughed. "No, you are not, but like many submissives, you seem only to have listened to the part of that rule that you wanted to hear. A Dominant may command both his own collared submissive and any submissive who consents to his command. Which, conveniently, you have." The Dominant instructor grinned wickedly. "So suck. Or be dismissed."

Delia growled in frustration and dropped to her knees beside the stupid teddy bear. It was wide, and she looked for somewhere to put her hands to brace herself as she leaned over the side of its torso. Unfortunately, in order to reach the bear's cock, she had to put her hands on its fuzzy body. The stuffed creature smushed beneath her palms and fingers. It felt soft—too soft, its body sinking to the floor beneath her weight—and not warm like a person would. She didn't like it.

She leaned over to get the humiliating part of this research over with. Although, as her lips parted to touch the rubbery dong, she realized that any part of fucking a teddy bear was the humiliating part of this research. She closed her eyes and pretended it was a real cock she was readying for her ass. The taste of rubber destroyed the illusion. The strong taste almost made her gag. She slobbered over it as much as she could, getting it wet.

Master Caspius clucked his tongue at her. "Come, now. Make it look sexy."

She side-eyed him and huffed air through her nose. But she stuck her tongue out and started running it up and down the length of the cock, boring through Master Caspius with an intense squint of the eyes as she did. The instructor laughed in delight. "So angry. So defiant."

She bit her teeth against the bear's dildo.

"Now, now. That's no way to behave. I think you're done with your little treat." Master Caspius tapped his black cane against the floor. "Mount the bear."

She turned away from him so she wouldn't have to look at his face and squatted over the teddy bear's crotch, lining up the dildo to put it in her ass.

"No, no. Not there. Put the bear's cock in your cunt."

She made an exasperated sound. "What! Why? I thought I was an assistant for anal techniques. That's what I came here for."

"You are an assistant for anal techniques. And what you came here for is to serve me. So listen, and do as I've said. You really are horrible at submission."

Delia clenched her teeth together, feeling every muscle in her jaw tighten. How dare he. She sat down on the dildo, letting it slide into her cunt, feeling her warm, slightly sticky drool smearing against her labia. "Why did you have me get it wet if I was just going to put it in my cunt? It can lubricate itself, you know."

"I wanted to watch you suck the bear's cock. Simple as that."

She couldn't see the instructor's face with her back to him, but she imagined he had that big, annoying grin on his face again.

"Go ahead and fuck the bear, little submissive one."

Teeth gritted together again, Delia began to move her hips against the teddy bear. At least it was wide enough that it provided a bit of padding for her knees against the hard floor in the secluded research room. The room was in the campus library and was one of several rooms that provided places for private study. When she realized, feeling the dildo press against her engorged g-spot, that she was somewhat aroused, she felt annoyed with herself and focused on fucking the stupid bear harder, taking out her frustration on it.

"Yes, that's good," Master Caspius said. "Now, stop. Wait right there and keep the dildo in."

She stopped, a scowl on her face, her mouth turned downward, as she stared at the blank, expressionless eyes of the teddy bear. Then she felt Master Caspius slide in behind her on the bear.

"What the hell?"

"Ah, ah, stay."

Master Caspius wrapped his knees around her thighs. He put his hands on her hips. "Bend forward a bit, please."

She lifted her hips up off the wet fur beneath her.

"Not too much. Keep the dildo in."

She sighed at his constant instruction. Then she gasped as the instructor pressed his hard cock into her ass hole, placing one hand around her and grabbing onto her cunt to push her back onto him as he sunk his whole cock into her ass. She felt resistance, as the dildo took up part of the space inside her. She could feel the instructor's cock pressing against the dildo through the thin wall between her cunt and her ass. She panted at the intense sensation of being stuffed. Then, without time to even adjust to the new sensation, Master Caspius began fucking her from behind, both of them sitting knees spread on the bear.

The instructor immediately began moaning. She wondered what it felt like for him, with the dildo rubbing up against his cock through the thin wall in her body. He didn't take it easy on her. He was fucking her relentlessly, thrusting upward into her. With his cock stuffing her ass, the dildo pressed even harder against her g-spot, and it was making her cunt leak all over the bear. She was getting coarse, little hairs stuck to her cunt and her inner thighs. In addition to her g-spot getting constant pressure, Master Caspius's cock was reaching deep into her belly, hitting the spot in there that always made her squirt. Delia gasped in tiny breaths. Her eyes rolled back in her head. She'd never felt anything so intense. And then just like that, Master Caspius grunted, wrapping his arms around her and pressing her body into his as his cock pulsed inside her. She was left unfinished, cunt weeping fluids.

He stayed behind her like that for a moment, panting against her back. Then, he let go of her and pulled his still very hard dick out of her ass, making her suck in a breath. The small dildo left in her cunt suddenly felt as though there was nothing inside her at all.

She looked back over her shoulder. "Is that all? We're done already?"

The instructor gave her his wicked grin. "Had to get the first one out of the way. I intend to fill your servile little ass several more times this evening."

Delia wasn't entirely sure if she was angry at him for the way he was talking to her or relieved at the prospect that she would be able to get off tonight. She was certain, however, that she was pissed that the decision was in Master Caspius's hands. Still, that's what she signed up for, so she may as well start getting used to it. Plus, she was attracted to the instructor, and the chances of getting a position in his household when she graduated were likely slim, so she might as well enjoy his cock and his lightning aura for as long as she could. As she got up and tried to wipe the curly little bear hairs from her sticky inner thighs, she wondered if the Dominant she ended up with after graduation would be anything like Master Caspius.

Her thoughts were broken by the instructor calling over to her. "You. Get over here." She gritted her teeth together as she turned around and walked toward the other side of the room, where the instructor stood at a wooden table. Her lack of orgasm thus far was making her irritable, especially since her ass felt the lingering effects of being used. She pressed her lips together and focused on her breathing, steeling herself not to retort to anything Master Caspius said to her.

She looked up into his eyes and said, "Mmhmm?" through pressed together lips.

"I have some materials for you to take with you tonight for studying." A box lay in front of the instructor on the table. It was fairly long, the size of box that perhaps a fiddle could fit into. He lifted the lid. Inside was a set of disturbingly large butt plugs. At the look on her face, Master Caspius grinned wickedly. "Let's see what you can really do with that ass."

For a moment, she felt speechless. Then she felt the pressure rise in her head. "What the fuck is wrong with you? How am I supposed to put those inside my body?"

He lifted a hand into the air and shrugged. "That's your problem, not mine."

"I've already taken the largest plug in the training set. Nobody could put one of these into their ass."

Master Caspius looked down at her in derision. "You took the largest plug in a training set for novices. Many people, in fact, have taken larger. I have submissives in my own household who are perfectly capable of inserting even the largest of these three plugs."

Delia felt shocked. Her mouth dropped open, staring at the enormous butt plugs inside the box. They were not steel, thank goodness. The box would have been a burden to carry if they were. Instead, each was made of a different color of highly polished wood. Still, she felt skeptical that people were putting these monsters into their asses.

The instructor continued speaking. "As I've told you before, and still stands, if you refuse to practice with the plugs, you can see yourself out of my research."

She was half-inclined to tell him to forget it, but one thing he said prickled her. "If submissives in your household can take these plugs, then I can." She crossed her arms over her chest.

Master Caspius chuckled. "I knew you would say so."

"Should I start practicing with them now?"

The instructor let the lid of the box fall, snapping closed. "Certainly not. Practice is for your own time. I won't have you wasting mine. Now bend over and grab your ankles, and do not let go of them, no matter what."

CHAPTER FOURTEEN

Monsters in the Dark

When Delia got back to her dorm room, her ass felt like it had been permanently gaped, and she couldn't tighten it enough to prevent Master Caspius's cum from seeping out and dripping down her legs. She'd gotten to come, though, and her cunt felt satisfied. She removed the long, wooden box from under her arm and laid it across the top of her dresser. It wouldn't fit in the drawers.

Meela was lying on her bed, reading from a textbook. She peered up over the pages, eyebrows raised. "What you got there?"

Delia cleared her throat. "Apparently, my ass is not stretched quite to Master Caspius's expectations." She flopped the lid open, revealing the three monster plugs inside.

Meela tossed the textbook aside, jumped up, and came over to her. "Ooo, that is so exciting!"

"Exciting? What the hell are you talking about? How am I supposed to get one of these things into my ass?"

"It's fun stretching your limits."

Delia eyed her friend. "How far, exactly, have you 'stretched' your limits?"

Meela blushed and looked down at the floor. "Come here and let me show you something."

Meela walked over to her own dresser and kneeled down on the ground to access the bottom-most of the three drawers. When she pulled it open, there were a bunch of individually-wrapped bundles of various sizes inside. Meela pulled one of them out, holding the bundle in her hands. It was about the size of a cantaloupe. Meela balanced the hefty object on one hand as she unwrapped it with the other.

Inside was a turquoise butt plug ringed in ridges that wrapped around its circumference. It was bigger than any of the new plugs Delia had brought home. Meela held it up and blushed. "This is the prize of my collection."

"Holy shit, Meela. You use that thing?"

"Oh, yes. The ridges feel amazing. And they help hold the lube in."

"What else do you have in that drawer?"

Meela began pulling bundles out of her dresser and laying them on her bed. The dildos were monsters. Literally. They weren't just long and girthy, they were inhuman. Her friend had dildos that looked like minotaur cocks, dildos that looked like werewolf cocks, dildos that looked like the tentacles of creatures from the beyond, a dragon cock, and even one that was a scaled-down, floppy, whale penis. For being her shy, quiet friend, Meela had a lot of unexpected kinks hiding in that drawer. In fact, Delia was starting to feel a little dull in comparison. Or at least inexperienced.

"Why do you have all these?"

"Like I said, I collect them. They're beautiful, aren't they?"

Delia nodded. She had to admit that some of them were really well-crafted. Much more visually appealing than the plain, boring plugs that come in the training sets.

"How did I not know that you had these?"

Meela blushed again. "Well, I never use them when anyone else is around."

That checked out. As wild as Meela's interests might be, she never could bring herself to perform in front of others. After viewing Meela's collection, Delia suddenly had a renewed sense of determination at working her way through the new training set. With Meela's help, she might even be able to show Master Caspius a few things he hadn't thought of.

"All right. Well, I'm going to go stretch my ass with a new butt plug while it's still opened up from helping Master Caspius with his research."

"I'm so glad you were able to get a position with him after all."

Delia laughed. "If it were an option, you definitely would have beat me out for this position, too." Then she frowned and looked at her friend. "Why don't you let anyone know about your talents? They would really help you out when it's time to get a permanent position."

Meela shrugged. "I'll be fine. I'm practicing other skills that will help me to stand out." Meela didn't sound all that confident, but Delia didn't want to push the issue. Meela had helped her so much. When she'd finished her research with Master Caspius, she promised herself that she would find a way to help Meela get over her shyness and secure herself a good position after graduation. They still had a couple years of training left. The thought of someone as amazing as Meela going to waste was unacceptable to her.

First, however, she had mini-monster number one to tackle.

Delia spent the next hour coaxing the big butt plug into her ass. She was starting to think that maybe she was nearing her maximum stretching capacity, but it did eventually go in all the way, and she felt extremely full with it inside her. At this point, though, it wasn't really much of a sexy sensation anymore. Mostly she just felt satisfaction at the achievement. But she really didn't see the point of putting such large things in her ass. No one had a cock that big.

Sure, for Meela it made sense. She was shy. She probably preferred playing by herself. But Delia was fine showing off in front of someone else, and she liked what a real cock could do. It wasn't like she planned to spend her time alone with a toy collection, so she didn't really understand the point of this new practice. She prepared herself to squeeze out the extra large plug and shuddered as it slurped out of her hole. Then she gave her ass hole a few practice squeezes to tighten it back up to a closer-to-normal size and got ready for bed. She had another research session with Master Caspius after her classes tomorrow.

CHAPTER FIFTEEN

Getting Loose

The library was quiet and dark as Delia made her way to the private study rooms. The sun was already going down, but the candles weren't all lit yet. After her talk with Meela last night, she had a renewed sense of respect for this building. As she walked, she noted the sheer numbers of books on the tall, wide shelves to either side of her. Each of those books contained knowledge about kinks, fetishes, and sexuality that she potentially hadn't encountered yet. She had felt like she knew everything, but she hardly knew anything at all. Rather than feel dwarfed by this knowledge, she felt excited.

This was different for her. Normally, she felt insecure whenever she felt like she wasn't the best, but after seeing Meela's collection, and as she gazed at the vast quantities of books, she realized that nobody was the best. Not really. Not even Master Caspius, much as he might know.

She entered the room at the back of the library, closing the door quietly behind her. Master Caspius was already waiting inside. He was fully clothed, though his gloves were off. He'd laid them on the table.

"How was your practice session with the new plugs?"

"Humbling," she answered.

"No luck, then?"

"I got the first one in."

"That's excellent to hear. Let us begin today's research, then." Master Caspius moved aside, and Delia saw that he had placed a pile of soft blankets in the floor. "Remove your tunic and lie down."

"Stomach or back?"

"On your back, please."

Master Caspius had tried out all kinds of positions with her yesterday, and the prospect of merely lying on her back—at least to start—sounded like a relief. Delia pulled the loose tunic up over her head, tossed it onto the floor, and laid down.

"Put your knees up and spread your legs."

She did so.

"Now, let's see how well your new training plugs have prepared you."

She probably should have felt alarmed at that statement, but at this point, hardly anything the instructor pulled out could have surprised her.

The instructor dipped his fingers into a tin of lubricating balm and began rubbing it against her sensitive ass hole. She closed her eyes, relaxing against the blankets, and enjoyed having an easy task for a while. Master Caspius pressed two fingers against her ass and inserted them, rubbing the lubricant around inside her. She had really grown to love anal sex, and just the two fingers felt really good, massaging inside her ass.

The instructor added more lubricant and added a third finger. He did not fuck her hard with his fingers. He simply kept massaging them into her. It felt oddly gentle, almost sensuous, of Master Caspius. Then, after the next time the instructor applied more lube, she felt his fingers change formation. Master Caspius had bunched together all of his fingers, and his thumb, into a single unit, and she felt him press this bunch of digits against her ass hole. She tensed up. Then she realized that was probably the worst thing she could do, and she exhaled, letting her knees fall further apart.

Of all the things she thought Master Caspius might try with her, she had not anticipated this. His bunched-together fingers began probing into her ass, easing their way in bit by bit. It felt strange.

There were more edges to a group of fingers than a smooth plug or dildo. It didn't hurt, though. Her ass stretched easily enough after all the training it had been through. She was grateful, however, for Master Caspius's slender fingers.

The instructor pressed his fingers into her until he reached the ridge of the knuckles. There, he met some resistance. The instructor then took his free hand and used it to slather more lubricant around her stretched-out hole, massaging it in near his knuckles. At that point, Delia opened her eyes and looked down. She was too shocked at what she saw, however, to react before it was done. Master Caspius grabbed his own wrist with his free hand and shoved the rest of his hand inside her, forcing the knuckles past her opening. She gasped and tensed up, but only after his entire hand had forced its way into her ass hole. Her ass squeezed against his wrist. It was almost like having a butt plug inside her, with the narrower handle sticking out. She squeezed her ass around Master Caspius's wrist again, intentionally this time, feeling her muscles flutter against the hand inside her.

Then he began to move the fist around inside her. It was thicker than his cock, and it was still warm flesh. It felt intense, and she had the feeling back that she had gotten when she first started this anal adventure—the feeling of doing something deviant, something her body was never intended for and yet perfectly suited to. She began to writhe in pleasure as his hand massaged inside her. Master Caspius put one hand on her thigh, pressing her leg up off the ground and holding it in the air, and he slowly began sliding his forearm in and out, pistoning his fist in her ass.

The instructor leaned forward a bit, putting some leverage into his thrusting. With every thrust, half his forearm went inside her. Master Caspius's fist and arm were thicker and longer than any cock she'd ever taken. And her ass swallowed it up greedily. The instructor sped up the movement of his arm, fucking her fast and deep. As she looked down, she could see the bulge of his fist in her abdomen, moving inside her belly in waves. She moaned and licked her lips. She'd never seen anything so hot in her life. The things her body could do was amazing.

She couldn't help it; as Master Caspius relentlessly pumped his fist into her, she started to squirt. Small trickles at first, and then she was squirting fountains into the air. The squirt hit Master Caspius in the chest, pulse after pulse of fluids until she was writhing on the blankets. When she was done, the instructor stopped fisting her but kept his arm, halfway up the forearm, inserted in her ass.

He ran a finger from his free hand around her stretched-out rim. "Hmm...I wonder what else I could fit in here. I don't think you've hit your limit yet. You enjoyed that too much."

There was a knock at the door, and Master Caspius looked back over his shoulder. "A moment, please."

The instructor turned back to Delia. "Unfortunately, what I have planned for the remainder of our research tonight is unlikely to stretch you more than a fisting, but you should be nice and warmed up for it."

Slowly, the instructor pulled his arm out of her ass. A final trickle of squirt dripped down her cunt. It felt like his arm was three feet long as it slid out of her, leaving her stretched hole feeling loose and empty. Then, Master Caspius stood up and went to the door, leaving Delia a wet, sweaty mess on the pile of blankets.

The instructor opened the door to the private study room. Delia expected him to simply answer a question for whoever was at the door, but instead, the stranger walked right into their private room. She slapped her thighs together and crossed her arms over her chest. She didn't mind giving a show, but she didn't even know who this person was.

Except that as she looked closer, she realized that she did know them. They were wearing a suede black cloak over their clothes, like many of the Dominant instructors, but the hood was down. It was Mistress Deblis. The Instructor of Pegging must have just come in from outside. Delia relaxed a bit against the blankets and saw that Mistress Deblis carried a large, black bag.

Master Caspius closed the door behind the other Dominant instructor. "Thank you for coming to assist with research this evening, Mistress Deblis."

"My pleasure. I found this initiate to be quite accommodating when she assisted my class."

Something about the way the Dominant instructors discussed her while she was lying right there bristled Delia, but she said nothing. She merely got up and started wiping herself off with a nearby towel. As she dried herself, she watched Mistress Deblis lay her big, black bag on the table and open it. She pulled out something like a pillow and unfolded it. Unfolded, it appeared to be a small, thin mattress. The Dominant instructor left this lying on the tabletop and pulled out a red, leather harness from the bag, which she began to fasten over her pants.

Master Caspius gave Mistress Deblis a look. "Better not leave your pants on." He gestured to his own shirt. "This one squirts." Then Master Caspius pulled his shirt off over his head, hanging it on the back of a chair. The Instructor of Anal Technique stood completely naked. Delia rarely saw Dominants completely naked. Master Caspius didn't seem to mind, though. The man appeared just as cocky without his clothes on, standing with his hands on his hips.

Mistress Deblis glanced over at Delia toweling herself off and removed the harness she'd been buckling on. She unlaced her black, leather pants and shimmied them over her hips before pulling them off each of her legs. Then she wrapped the straps of the harness back around her hips and thighs, fastening the metal buckles. When the Instructor of Pegging was done preparing herself, she lifted her bag off the table and sat it on the floor. Mistress Deblis gestured to Delia. "Come on over here."

Delia walked over, nude and feeling cold after the squirt had evaporated from her skin.

"Master Caspius, I'll allow you to be on bottom today."

Master Caspius nodded to Mistress Deblis, understanding her request, though Delia didn't know what they meant. Master Caspius walked over to the table and laid down on his back on top of the thin, unfolded mattress. He was at the edge of the table so that his legs hung over. The Instructor of Anal Technique began stroking his cock, getting it hard.

"All right, Delia." The Instructor of Pegging turned toward her. "You're going to straddle and mount Master Caspius."

Delia walked over to the table and reached a knee up. She realized it was a bit high to climb comfortably, so she grabbed one of the wooden chairs in the room and pulled that over next to the tabletop. Then she climbed onto the seat of the chair and up onto the table, kneeling next to Master Caspius. She raised one knee over him, straddling him with a knee on either side. She began to lower herself and then paused.

"Is this a double penetration exercise? Should I mount him with my cunt?"

Mistress Deblis laughed. "It is, in fact, a double penetration exercise."

Delia started to lower herself, and then Mistress Deblis interjected. "But no, you should not mount him with your cunt. Stick Master Caspius's cock in your ass."

Delia nodded. She sank her ass down onto Master Caspius's fully erect cock. It went in easily, as stretched as she was. Still, it felt good having something inside her ass. She sighed pleasantly as the cock penetrated her.

Mistress Deblis came up behind her and laid a hand on one of her ass cheeks. "All right. Now stay right there."

Master Caspius spread his legs apart beneath her, causing her own legs to spread slightly further apart. From behind her, she felt the smooth sensation of Mistress Deblis's dildo pressing between her cheeks. She gasped as the Instructor of Pegging pressed her slick dildo against the top of Delia's ass hole. Master Caspius moaned as the dildo pressed against his rigid cock. Then, with a few moments of pressure, Mistress Deblis's dildo popped inside, filling Delia's ass hole up with two separate cocks.

She now felt just as full as she had with Master Caspius's fist inside her. It was a delicious fullness. She also felt Master Caspius's cock throbbing at the pleasant sensation he must also be experiencing. Mistress Deblis began thrusting into her ass, the dildo pleasuring Delia's ass and frotting with Master Caspius's cock at the same time. Master Caspius lay still beneath her, moaning, enjoying the sensations. Occasionally, his hips would rock up and down, as though he were unaware that he'd begun thrusting.

Delia was in bliss with the two cocks stretching her ass open. She loved the feel of the two warm bodies pressing into her. She knelt on the table, eyes closed, and, despite her subordinate position to these two instructors, felt like a fucking goddess. For a moment, she forgot that she was here as an assistant and imagined the two Dominants servicing her, filling her for her own whims. As her orgasm came again—quicker this time both because of the fantasy in her mind and because she was already sensitive from the first round—she called out loudly, letting her pleasure loose from deep within her body.

Delia didn't squirt this time, but she felt something else let loose inside her. She felt something freed. Right now, she didn't give a fuck what either Master Caspius or Mistress Deblis wanted. She didn't care about serving them or whether they got off from this. Right now, Delia was experiencing true pleasure purely for herself.

"Fuck me harder, bitch," she called out as another orgasm neared.

Mistress Deblis slowed behind her but did not stop thrusting entirely. Delia bent over on her hands and knees, feeling the slow dildo thrusts go deeper inside her. She opened her eyes and stared into Master Caspius's face. She grinned wickedly. Delia had an idea for how to expand her own studies. And she realized that she owed all of this to herself. Sure, the epiphany had come from the research she'd done with Master Caspius, but she'd have never ended up here if it hadn't been for her own stubborn persistence.

CHAPTER SIXTEEN

Fuck Your Monster

"You said what to them?" Meela kneeled on her bed, staring across the room at Delia.

Delia laughed, hardly believing it herself. "I said, 'Fuck me harder, bitch!'"

"I can't believe you said that!"

"I know!"

"What did they do?"

Delia shrugged. "Mistress Deblis just kept fucking me until Master Caspius called the session over."

"So she listened to you?"

"Not exactly. She didn't fuck me harder. In fact, she slowed down. It was kind of annoying, but it still felt good anyway."

Meela's mouth hung open from across the room. "And then what happened?"

"They both told me that if I were their own collared sub, I would be in serious trouble and likely put into extended chastity." She grinned. "But I'm not their collared sub, and I'm not enrolled in their college, so they really can't do anything to me."

"You just got away with it?"

Delia nodded.

"Yes, but that's not the best part."

"There's more?"

"Not more to what happened. The best part is I got a great idea while I was sandwiched in between the two Doms. I realized that it could be a lot of fun to practice more with the other submissives. After all, after we graduate and get permanent positions in a household, we probably won't be permitted to have whatever kind of sex we want with whoever we want."

"That is an interesting idea."

"Speaking of which, you and I have played together, but only to help me practice at anal. How about I top you tonight?"

Meela blushed and pulled her blanket up to below her chin. "That's really nice of you to offer, but you don't have to."

"I know I don't have to. I want to. But if you don't, that's okay. I just thought it would be fun."

Meela tightened her grasp on the blanket. "No! I want to!"

Delia cocked an eyebrow at her. "You sure?"

"Yes." Meela was starting to look excited. "In fact, I know just which toy I'd like to use."

Delia giggled. "Excellent. I was hoping we might get to try out one of your special pieces."

Meela got up and went over to her dresser, squatting and pulling out one of the largest toys in the bottom drawer. As she laid it on the bed and began unwrapping it, Delia began to grin. The toy selected was the long, thick, tentacle-shaped dildo. This was going to be fun. Then she bit her lip, realizing she'd never pegged anyone before. Her worry lasted for all of a second. Oh well, she figured, I'll figure it out.

Meela pulled out her homemade rope harness and held it out to Delia. "May I?"

Delia nodded, standing over her kneeling friend, who began to tie the harness around her hips and thighs. She looked down at beautiful, dark-haired Meela on her knees and felt a touch of authority enter her. She rarely, at her height, stood over anyone. To have someone on their knees, catering to her, was something she'd never experienced before. Meela finished tightening the rope around Delia's lower body, and then she grabbed the floppy dong off the bed, strapping it into the rope harness.

"This one's kind of heavy. It takes extra rope." Meela continued wrapping rope around the dildo and weaving it through the hip harness. Delia watched the whole process with interest, noting where the frictions of the rope crossed. As Meela let go of the dildo and let the ropes take more of the weight, Delia could feel the heft of the large toy hanging off her. She looked down at it. It was grayish-colored with a rubbery texture. The gray swirled, in places looking lighter or darker. In some places, the dildo even had a few raised bumps to imitate suckers. She imagined those felt interesting.

"Okay, you're all ready to go."

Meela stood up, and Delia grabbed her new cock in her hands, feeling the weight of it and how it moved. She grinned. "Yes, I am."

Meela blushed and trotted over to the bed, quickly lying down and burying her face in the pillow. Her voice came out muffled. "Okay, I'm ready, too."

Delia couldn't help grinning at her friend still being so shy. She went over to her own bed and grabbed an extra pillow, and she returned to Meela's bed. "Here, let's prop you up a bit." She stuck the pillow under Meela's hips, raising her friend's butt up in the air. She ran her hands over Meela's butt. It felt like the softest suede under her hands. Then, she lubed up the massive tentacle and began sliding it up and down between Meela's ass cheeks. Her friend moaned into the pillow. Meela turned her head to the side, and Delia could see that her friend had her eyes closed and was biting her lower lip.

With one hand, she spread Meela's cheeks apart to reveal her puckered hole, and with the other, she pressed two lubricant-slicked fingers into that pucker, getting the rim wet and feeling how easily she'd be able to enter as her fingers slid inside. She knew Meela was obsessed with butt stuff, so she didn't waste her time. She grabbed onto the flexible end of the tentacle dildo and pressed it into her friend's ass. Meela responded by spreading her legs further apart and pushing her butt further into the air. Delia grinned. She loved how eager Meela was.

She fed the tentacle into Meela's ass with her hand, slowly getting enough of it inside the other woman that she could begin to apply pressure with her hips. When she encountered the first row of suckers, she watched as the ass in front of her gulped them inside, and Meela made pleasant little sighs with each gulp. Now using her hips,

Delia continued to steadily feed the tentacle into Meela's ass, and her friend took whatever she gave. The tentacle was about halfway inside, and Delia looked down at Meela's pleasantly stretched ass hole. She ran a finger around the stretched-out rim. Then she grasped Meela's hips in her hands and began rocking her own hips forward.

With each thrust, the tentacle buried itself a little bit further into Meela's ass. Delia could imagine what it must feel like, and she felt her cunt throbbing and drooling as she continued to work the tentacle further inside. The idea of getting the whole, huge thing inside of Meela turned her on insanely. She began thrusting faster, and Meela's ass opened up for her, taking in the final inches of the creature-cock, sucking it in.

Delia slapped her hips against Meela's ass, imagining that tentacle up inside her. She moved one hand around to feel Meela's belly as she fucked her, and sure enough, she could feel a bulge from the tentacle pumping inside Meela's abdomen. That turned her on even more, knowing how deep inside Meela she was, how fully she owned the other woman right now. She removed her hand and put it back onto Meela's hip, grasping the woman beneath her even tighter, fucking her mercilessly.

Meela moaned and drooled onto the pillow. Her pretty fists clenched the bedsheets, and her cheek rubbed against the pillow roughly with each thrust. Delia was breathing heavily. "Get up on your hands and knees," she said to Meela.

As Meela got into position, Delia stopped thrusting and, hands firmly on the other woman's hips, began pulling Meela's hips down onto the tentacle-cock, making Meela fuck herself on the monster-sized dildo. Delia could see a wet spot on the sheets, where Meela's cunt had drooled on them as she'd been laying down. She wondered how badly her secretly-slutty friend wanted that tentacle.

She let go of Meela's hips. "Stay right there." And then, Delia changed position, keeping the tentacle engulfed in Meela's stretched-out ass. She laid down on her back, putting her legs out straight between Meela's legs. "Now fuck your monster."

Delia watched as Meela knelt over the massive tentacle and began to fuck it, her ass bouncing up and down in front of Delia's face. With each pump, Meela sat all the way down on the dildo, slapping her ass cheeks against Delia's hips. Delia had a much better view in this position, and she watched the gray tentacle slither out of Meela's ass and slurp back inside. Meela moaned and pounded her ass down on the tentacle, and then Delia watched as her friend's body heaved and shuddered, orgasming repeatedly as she planted herself on the sucker-lined cock.

When Meela was done, she slumped down, legs bent and out to her sides, tentacle still completely inside her. "That was so much better with the tentacle attached to a person."

Delia chuckled. "I bet."

Slowly, Meela started to get up. Delia watched as her friend's ass released the kraken-cock. The thing slid out of her, bit by bit, hanging out of Meela's ass as she stood up, until finally, the last, wobbly inch slipped out of Meela's gaping hole and flopped over onto Delia's thigh. She could see her friend's ass hole still yawning open.

Meela looked back over her shoulder and blushed. Delia grinned at her. "That was fun."

Meela nodded.

"Okay, go ahead and take this harness off me. I've got more personal experiments to perform."

Meela knelt down and started untying the ropes. Delia could have done it herself. She only would have needed to reverse the steps Meela had taken putting it on, but she could see that Meela was currently deep in a submissive headspace, and it felt nice to lay back and let the other woman do the work, especially since Meela was clearly enjoying providing service. This must be what the Doms felt like. She figured that Dominants probably enjoyed bossing people around and getting everything taken care of for them, but she hadn't considered that they might actually feel pleasure at seeing a submissive in their element. Delia relaxed, put her hands behind her head, and enjoyed the attention from her friend as she planned her next experiment.

CHAPTER SEVENTEEN

Yes, Ma'am

"Thanks for meeting up with me again, Instructor Pratom. I know I'm not exactly one of your best students. I've been distracted this semester."

"It's no problem at all, Delia. And you've certainly been applying yourself to your pursuits, if not in my class." Instructor Pratom chuckled. "To be honest, I was a little surprised that you asked for my help. I'd heard that you'd secured a research position with Master Caspius."

"Yes, I have. I've simply developed some additional research interests."

"Good. I like to see initiates pursuing their talents."

Delia eyed Instructor Pratom. He wore a soft, loose pair of cotton trousers and a short, cream-colored tunic. "Okay, here's what I'd like you to do for me. Lie down on your desk and take off your pants."

"Right to the point, just like last time, I see."

"Yes, I'm eager to practice something particular."

"Anything I need to know before we get started?"

"No, it won't be anything too challenging for you—as long as you're able to maintain your chastity while I experiment."

"No worries there. I've developed a series of breathing exercises to help me not to come. I hope my lack of ejaculation doesn't offend you."

Delia shrugged and grinned. "Well, we're not really here for your pleasure, are we?"

The instructor looked at her curiously. "True enough." Instructor Pratom removed his pants and sat down on the edge of the desk, easing himself down onto his back.

"Get yourself hard, instructor."

While Instructor Pratom began touching his cock, Delia pulled her tunic off over her head and laid it on the floor, leaving herself only in her thigh-high socks and low boots. She watched in amazement as Instructor Pratom once again brought himself to full functionality within a matter of seconds. She'd never seen anyone get fully hard as fast as he did. She loved it, and she wondered at what kind of training his Dominant had done to get him to this point.

As soon as Instructor Pratom was ready, Delia pulled a chair up next to the desk. Her short stature made her feel momentarily insecure, but she pushed that feeling aside. That was the last thing she wanted to feel right now. Holding her chin up, she stepped up onto the chair and stood there, looking down at Instructor Pratom. She saw his dick flex under her gaze. After running her eyes over his body, she got onto the desk and kneeled over him. She wanted to take her time with this, so she stayed raised up over him, one knee on each side of his body. He looked rather vulnerable lying there with only a short tunic covering the top half of his body and no pants below.

Delia lowered herself onto him, sitting right on top of his rigid cock. She began to glide her already-wet cunt over it, her lips engulfing it on either side, sliding over it. Then she leaned forward slightly and started grinding her clit against Instructor Pratom's dick. It felt good. She leaned further forward, putting her hands on his chest and pressing her weight into him as she ground against him, using his body.

Delia humped her clit against the instructor's captive cock until she came, crying out sounds of pleasure. It was only a small orgasm — a warmup for the main event. She rocked forward and felt the tip of Instructor Pratom's cock touch the opening of her vagina, and she pressed against it, her hands still pressing her weight against his chest, her pussy engulfing his cock in one swallow. The instructor's cock sank inside her, and she sighed at the feeling. She let his dick sit there for a moment, soaking motionlessly, before slowly sliding her cunt up and down the length of him three times, squeezing her muscles on every upward movement so that it felt like her pussy was sucking on him. Then, she let his cock out of her cunt's grasp and pushed it back to her ass hole.

She looked down into Instructor Pratom's eyes and relished the look she saw there—another submissive put into their headspace of adoration and service. As she pressed his moistened cock into her ass, she grabbed up a handful of his tunic and gripped it like tightly-held reins. Then, she proceeded to pound Instructor Pratom into submissive oblivion, gritting her teeth, gripping his top, and slapping her ass into him as she fucked him.

Instructor Pratom had closed his eyes, clearly going through his breathing exercises to maintain his vow of chastity. Delia enjoyed knowing he had to work for it. She took her eyes off his face and closed her own eyes, tilting her head back and moaning. She pulled on Pratom's tunic, feeling her ass swallow the length of his cock over and over again.

She looked back down at him. The submissive instructor almost looked like he was meditating, the way that he was breathing.

"Don't come. Don't come, instructor. I'm not done with you yet."

Pratom let out a long, shuddering exhale and nodded his head, keeping his eyes squeezed closed. "Yes, Ma'am."

Delia startled at the term of authority. Then, a smile slid over her face. "That's right." She closed her eyes and rode the submissive instructor's cock. As she rode him, she lifted her hips high—not quite high enough for his cock to slip out, but almost. Then she plunged the whole thing back into her ass at once, enjoying the sensation of taking in the whole length of it. Enjoying knowing that this cock, for this moment in time, was hers to use as she wanted. She plunged the cock into herself again and again, until her clit clenched and she squirted out her orgasm all over Pratom's torso and tunic. She was always amazed at how much fluid came out of her when she squirted. When her squirt splattered onto him, the instructor's eyes flew open, looking down at the fluids flooding over his body. He gritted his teeth, but it didn't look like he didn't like it.

After she came, she kept riding the instructor, her ass splashing in the mess she'd made all over him, and then she sat down, panting, to rest. "Good job, instructor."

Pratom laughed and closed his eyes, panting. "You certainly gave me a challenge."

"That's good. That's why I'm giving you a little break. I'm not quite done with you." She squeezed the muscles in her ass, contracting them around his swollen, tortured cock.

The instructor sucked in a breath. "I really don't think I can take anymore right now."

Delia clucked her tongue. "Instructor Pratom, that's really not very selfless of you. I thought you were an expert in that matter." Then, clutching a wad of his wet tunic in one hand, she began fucking him again, pumping his cock into her ass. She was so turned on that every downward thrust caused another stream of fluid to squirt from her body, pumping out of her like a hand-pumped well and splashing onto Pratom's body, rolling off onto his desktop.

Instructor Pratom groaned, his eyes rolling back into his head. He began to count out loud from one to ten and back down again as he breathed.

When Delia was done with Instructor Pratom, she wrapped herself in her cloak and left the main building on the submissive side of campus. It wasn't a long walk from the building where most of the classes were kept to the dormitory. She walked slowly, feeling the crisp air of the winter night hit her cheeks. She thought back to the day earlier in the semester, the day that had started this whole adventure. It had been colder then. This night was only just at freezing—just cold enough to make her step carefully in case she encountered any icy patches on the stone. Still, it was cold enough to remind her of the feeling she had had that day. Such intense pain. Such an intense challenge.

She laughed at the thought that she had ever considered changing her major. She was a masochist through and through, that was for sure. It was clear from her choices that she liked torturing herself. She left the path that led to the dormitory and made her way into the woods behind the buildings, following a small trail. She wasn't entirely sure where she was headed. She just didn't feel like going to sleep yet, and she wanted to keep feeling the cold air on her cheeks.

The night was clear, and moonlight shone through the branches of the trees. Most of the trees in the forest surrounding DS Academy were evergreens. They helped the university maintain a sense of privacy and remain hidden from the outside world. When Delia looked up at the trees, towering over her, she did feel protected. She sighed. When she had come here, she thought she knew what she wanted. It was clear to her now that she had no idea what she wanted. She didn't even know what half the options were. She was more naïve than she could have ever imagined. She wished there was a way that she could learn more, explore all the options available to her.

As she walked, she came up to a fork in the trail. The path to the left circled back around to the submissive dormitories. The path to the right took her up to the stream that ran through campus and past the main building of the College of Dominance. The stream snaked through the woods from a lake to the north. She stood between them, at the fork, and looked down at the "v" between her boots, where the trail she was on stopped and broke apart into two different paths. She couldn't choose. She didn't know where she wanted to go. She took a deep and stepped forward. Her boot touched gravel. She took another step, and her boot touched a soft layer of browned evergreen needles.

Delia picked up her pace, walking straight forward, taking neither of the paths. She marched right between the two of them. Whenever there was a tree in her way, she would veer around it, slightly to one side or the other. She kept moving, not knowing where she would end up. The cold was starting to get to her, and she thought about turning back, but she wasn't ready. Not yet. She walked faster, breath puffing out in front of her, nose starting to feel a little numb. She adjusted her scarf over her face and kept on.

Then, suddenly, she saw something. Something that was not just a part of the forest, but made by a person. It was a circle of stones. She glanced around and crept toward the stones. Various plants had sprung up in the circle, and layers of tree needles covered the inside of it, but it looked like it had once been the place of someone's campfire. Panting, she stepped into the circle and turned back to face the direction she had come. She sat down on the bed of soft tree needles inside the ring of stones. She wasn't the first person to wander off the trail. Someone else had been out here, forging their own path. That meant it could be done.

She jumped up, knowing that she had figured it out. She ran all the way back to the trail, her lungs burning with the icy air flowing into them. When she reached the fork, she took the path back to the dormitories. She kept running, laughing at the pain in her chest. By the time she got to the building, her lungs and face burned, and her lips were dried out and crinkled. She caught her breath in the entrance and made her way up to her room, throwing the door open.

Meela sat in bed, a book on her lap and a candle lit on her nightstand. The woman looked up at Delia in the doorway. "Where have you been?"

Delia ignored the question. It was probably obvious anyway since evergreen needles were still clinging to parts of her socks. She closed the door and pressed herself back against it, grinning at her friend. "I'm going to apply for admission to the College of Dominance."

"You're leaving the school?"

"No, no. I'm staying in the College of Submission."

Meela cocked her head, confused.

Delia strode over to her friend, grin widening. "I'm going to study both."

Meela carefully put her book down and stood up. "Why would you do that? Aren't you worried that you won't get a position if you're trained as a Dominant, too? Or..." Meela didn't seem to know what else to say.

Delia stopped grinning. She'd thought her friend would be excited. "I'm not worried about that."

The concern didn't leave Meela's eyes.

"Listen. I know what I'm doing. I have to do it. It's the only path for me."

Meela stepped forward and took one of Delia's hands in both of hers. "You know it's going to be a longer road for you, like this."

"I'm prepared for the journey."

Meela squeezed her hand and nodded. "Then I'm here for you."

Delia's grin returned. "Thank you. Now lie down and let me sit on your face. I'm horny."

More from B. B. Rattan

Find more from B. B. Rattan at www.patreon.com/bbrattan.

You can follow B. B. Rattan on Twitter @1bbrattan www.twitter.com/1bbrattan.